KADEN CONORICH

Starcrossed

To all the things that make us change

Chapter 1

I was already in his home by the time he walked in. My contacts faded from transparent lenses to an opaque black as he switched on the light, adjusting my eyes from the dark to the sudden brightness.

"Hello, Gordon."

He fumbled with his keys at the sound of my voice, doing a double take as my eyes returned to normal, making him question what he'd seen. Gordon was a thin man with thinning bleach blond hair who always wore the same red velvet track suit. A thin line of hairs lined his trembling upper lip, what some might generously call a mustache. Imposing was never a word that would be used in the same sentence as his name, but he still got his job done. Gordon also had a reputation for being a drug dealer who only associated with the most elite and exclusive customers. At least, he was supposed to.

"Oh, hi, Malice….err, sir." He laughed nervously. "What's up?"

I let him sit and think for a bit before I said anything else. "Gordon, when I hired you and your 'crew,' what was our agreement?"

"Oh. Like specifically or…"

"I'll remind you. I protect you. In return, you only sell to the one-percent scum I tell you to. We feed their corruption and fuel their inhibitions so the people see what they really are. Or they just OD. You only sell to people within those parameters, right?"

His body trembled, like a leaf in the wind, and a thin layer of sweat glistened on his skin. "Right, yeah. Of course."

I rose from my seat and gradually walked towards him. "So why were your guys seen dealing at a high school?"

His eyes moved around the room, trying to avoid looking at me. "Aw, I don't know. Maybe they went rogue. Or the rich scum got to 'em. I would never—"

I struck him with a length of chain from inside my black trench coat. Gordon crumpled against the wall and spat blood onto his carpet. I walked back towards his chair, grabbing the duffel bag I'd left beside it.

"See, I already talked to your men. They said you told them they could expand your business. Assuming I stay in the dark. Unfortunately for them, and you, I didn't."

Gordon just stared at the bag, seemingly unable to comprehend it.

"Go on," I said. "Open it."

He struggled with the zipper, finally pulling it open after an agonizing minute. As soon as it was open, Gordon stared in shock before vomiting straight into it. Not how I would have treated the decapitated heads of my associates, but to each their own.

The chain, fabricated from the living metal armor, now hidden as my clothing, curved and elongated into a sickle. Gordon stared wide-eyed at the blade.

"Please, boss. I'm sorry. I won't do it again."

"I know." I drove the tip of the blade into his jaw and pulled hard. His tongue lolled into the empty air as the lower half of his face disappeared. I flicked my wrist and his jaw bounced onto the floor. I let the pain reach him, and he tried to scream. Only a sad, blubbering noise came out. Another slash cut his throat, and I let him bleed. The sickle retreated into my jacket as I stepped over the blood and vomit, quietly exiting the apartment. I had unfinished business, and the night was just beginning.

Chapter 2

Tomorrow, a politician would open his new office. A gold plated monument built with avarice and set on a foundation of bribes and corruption. Possibly with actual bodies buried beneath it. But tonight, I would wreak havoc upon this building.

No ordinary bomb would suffice for this. I'd prepared something special for the occasion. Thirteen spheres, each containing a ravenous nanite horde. The nanites would consume certain segments, leaving enough of it to form a ruin. Once the building collapsed, they would melt into each other and fuse with the debris. The result would be a jagged scar that would render the site unusable. A warning to those in the same circles.

I pulled on the door that was supposed to be left unlocked for me and met with resistance. No matter; probably best for them anyway. And after all, this was about sending a message. The living metal on my right arm hardened. I leaned back and threw my fist forward, the force of the blow enhanced by my armor. Glass and twisted metal flew forward into the building, scattering across the marble floor. No alarms rang out, no metal shutters slammed shut over the doors and windows. Silent alarm then, but always being watched. Which was fine. I wanted them to know it was me. I removed the first of the containers from my jacket, a black cylinder with seven spheres. Two in the basement, two in the lobby, nine spread across the other floors.

A flash of light and the flutter of wings came from outside. I spun around and glanced out the window, catching a glimpse of white and gold. She was circling the building, wings beating fast and heavy. My time was up. I pressed my ring and middle fingers into my left palm, triggering my devices. I watched as the last sphere opened like a metal flower in bloom, releasing a pool of scuttling darkness. The nanites chewed through their surroundings and spread, shooting out in webs of black. A clatter of wood on the floor brought me out of the euphoria of watching my devices work. I turned to find a middle-aged custodian, face white with fear, shaking in the room's doorway he had just finished cleaning.

I let out a heavy sigh. "For fuck's sake."

Grabbing his arm as I sprinted past, I led the man down the stairwell, taking two steps at a time. While I had programmed the nanites to avoid anything with a heartbeat, the collapsing building couldn't care less. I heard glass shatter and feet hit the ground, echoing from the floor I was just on. *She thinks I just took a hostage.* No time to prove her wrong. The nanites grew from stringy webs to powerful tendrils crashing through the walls as we made our descent. Finally, the lobby came into view.

I led the custodian through the crumbling floor and tossed him through the me-sized opening that was gradually shrinking. I looked back as I crawled through the hole, catching one last glimpse of gold cut through the wreckage. Then it sealed shut. That was going to piss her off. But it gave me time to leave. I scowled at the custodian, letting a growl rise in my throat to remind him he should still fear me. Then I took off and began my walk home.

Chapter 3

"Home" was an abandoned Gothic cathedral, complete with twisting spires that reached for God and stained glass fixtures depicting some more gruesome bible scenes. To the left of the pulpit was my workstation, two tables forming a V, which held a mess of wires connecting a couple of computer towers to an unholy mass of monitors. Next to that, a third table hosted a collection of tools with one of my works in progress. Deeper in the building, I had set up my living area in the former priest's quarters, complete with a cot, portable shower, and one of those chemical toilets doomsday preppers loved.

I had shoved the original wooden podium down and replaced it with something of my own. Where it once stood was now a large glass tube, a metal base anchoring it to the floor, which held my living metal. The suit was a restless thing, constantly moving around its container, hanging from the sides with inky tendrils. I knelt before the container, my long dark hair hanging in front of my face, hands clasped as if in prayer. I'd even found a rosary to complete the look of the pious man. She would be here soon, and I had prepared.

It wasn't every day you got an audience with the Guardian Angel of Spire City. Well, it was more common in my line of work. Glass shattered behind me and fell to the floor, marking her arrival.

"Hello, Zarael. I see you and your ilk still have trouble with doors."

I propped myself up on one knee as the living metal flowed from its home. I embraced the icy darkness as it flowed over me, stretching and taking form. Sharp and twisted armor took shape. My hands turned into razor claws. A mask covered my mouth, turning my breathing into a sinister rasp. My contacts darkened again, turning my eyes into black mirrors. The last of the living metal formed a ragged, ever flowing cape, adding just a touch of dramatic flair. A necessary feature for any good supervillain.

I stood and turned to face her. Zarael hovered in the air, flaming sword in hand. She had a golden aura that cast a warm light over the shadows of the cathedral. She wore luminous golden armor, etched with a dead language, over a plain white tunic. Her ethereal hair was cut short and flowed like a halo as she hung in the air. She stared at me with gorgeous amber eyes as her pure white wings lowered her to the floor.

"Oh, poor Malice. Did I break a window in the building you're squatting in?" she said as she rubbed her finger and thumb together, playing the world's smallest violin.

I scowled beneath my mask and flicked my wrists, prompting the suit to form two sickles, dark energy crackling along their blades.

Zarael threw back her head and let out a sigh. "Time out. Can we just take a minute before we go all out? Even with Holy Flames, getting out of the mess you made took a lot out of me."

I lowered my weapons. "I suppose. There's no rule saying we have to fight right away."

Zarael ran her hand over her sword, causing the flames to

dissipate, and fell into one of the dusty pews that lined the cathedral floor. She looked around, studying my lair. "Where do you guys even find places like this?"

"There's an app," I replied.

"No shit."

Silence filled the room. I stood awkwardly, waiting for something to happen. Zarael just sat there, tapping her hands against the seat. After a few minutes, she met my gaze.

"Oh, I'm sorry. Did you wanna monologue or something?"

"Uh, sure." I finally let the sickles return to nothing. "As you know, a certain corrupt politician has made Spire City his new base of operations and built a massive tower—"

Zarael laughed. "That thing was huge! You think he was compensating for something?"

I stared at her. She cleared her throat. "Sorry, continue."

"As I was saying—"

"Actually, do you mind coming over here? There's an echo, and I keep hearing the same sentence twice."

I hesitated for a moment, unsure what to do. "Okay."

I moved down the row, eyeing her warily. Zarael moved over and patted the space next to her, smiling up at me. I sidestepped into the pew and pushed my cape back as I sat so it wouldn't get caught under me.

"Anyway—"

"Did I ever drop a building on you?"

"What?…No, I don't think so."

She nodded. "Oh, okay." She looked around the chapel again. "Kinda shitty thing to do. Just btdubs."

I adjusted myself in the pew. "Okay. Anyway—"

"Can I ask you a question?"

"Nothing seemed to stop you before."

"Why do you do this?"

"What?"

She gestured all around us. "All this. The supervillain stuff. What made Malice?"

I took a moment to think it over. "I've always been different, an outcast. From a young age, I was a loner. My nose was always stuck in a book, my interests were odd to the other kids. My parents accepted me how I was, though. But then my mother died. The factory she worked at ruled it an accident, but my father knew better. He took it upon himself to investigate, and his obsession consumed him. Then he died, worked himself to death. Or so they say. After that, they bounced me around from foster home to foster home, but it was never truly a home." I looked over at her. "That would've broken anyone else, but not me."

Zarael just nodded, clearly in awe of my dark history.

"So I vowed my vengeance on the society that killed the only people I loved. I vowed to cut out the corruption of this world. You may see me as a villain, but I am the hero that is needed."

I let this sink in. Just from the look on her face, I could tell Zarael was deep in thought.

"So wait, when does the suit come in?"

"What?"

"The suit, your suit. It's like an alien symbiote you bonded with, right?"

"No, I made this."

Zarael stood up fast enough that my sickles partially re-formed.

"So you're saying, you can make this…stuff that everyone thinks is some inhibition-blocking alien goo that makes you like…" She gestured at all of me. "…this, and you spend all your time blowing up buildings in weird, convoluted ways and bossing around drug dealers?"

"Everyone thinks it's an alien?"

Zarael pinched the bridge of her nose and shut her eyes like she had a migraine. "Not nearly the point. You even saved that janitor—"

"Custodian."

"Custodian earlier. Why are you doing this when you could be actually helping people?"

"I thought I just told you that."

Zarael sighed and leaned against the pew in front of us. "Look, I'm not saying you have to be a hero or anything, but it just seems like you're wasting your potential and using your own pain to justify hurting others."

I mulled it over, and, for the first time in a long while, felt ashamed. I stood up, apparently a little too fast and too close to Zarael. She let out a yelp of surprise and struck me square in the face with a super-powered punch, sending me flying back into the pew. I felt my vision swim as the edges of my sight filled with darkness and my suit melted off me.

Chapter 4

My head slammed against a metal wall, bringing me back to consciousness. I scanned my surroundings. It looked like Zarael had placed me in the care of the "proper" authorities. They had me chained and bound me in the back of a villain transport, a more heavily reinforced version of your typical prison bus. My suit had melted away when I was knocked unconscious, leaving me in a black tank top and jeans. My head pounded with each shake of the vehicle. It felt like they were taking me down the most torn-up road to the prison.

A familiar face sat across from me, bobbing with the bumps and jolts of the road. "Hello, Curtis."

The guard beamed at me. "Oh, hiya, Mr. Malice."

Curtis and I had an arrangement. He had shitty health insurance, so I didn't hurt him too much when I escaped. When we first met, back in the days of leather and guy liner, before the living metal could form a full suit, Curtis took care of me. Zarael went easier on me since I was just a street level bad guy, not yet graduated to supervillain. In those days, I endured the real beating after my plans were thwarted. The officers that held me, waiting for the transport, hated everything about me. I was trying to tear down their way of life. So, they tried to dissuade me. I was barely conscious when the transport finally arrived. Curtis had done what he could, cleaning and bandaging my wounds with the first aid kit he bought with his own money. The way he looked at me, he saw me as a person, not just a villain. Curtis was kind. If more people had been kind like him, someone like me wouldn't have existed.

"How's your head? Z said she knocked you pretty good."

I gave him a quick smile to show I was okay. "I'll live. It was just a little sucker punch."

Curtis reached into his pocket and pulled out a bottle of painkillers. He dropped a few in my hand, and I closed my eyes as I popped them in and waited for them to take effect.

"How'd that tutor end up working out for your daughter?"

"Fantastic! She's actually looking forward to math now."

"See? Sometimes teachers just suck. Especially math teachers."

We couldn't help but laugh at that. I let out a heavy sigh as the laughter died down.

"Sorry, friend, I'll have to rough you up a little more tonight. Apparently, I'm not evil enough for Zarael."

Curtis shot me a look. "Something tells me she didn't say that. Also, I thought it was the alien suit that made you evil. That's why you're nicer when it's off."

Fuck you, Curtis.

I gave him a strained smile. "One, it's not alien. And two…" I snapped my handcuffs apart as the suit reformed over me. "It's not completely off of me."

***

I walked away from the wreckage of the villain transport, fuming at what had quickly become tonight's theme. Whatever.

Tomorrow I would go back to the cathedral and retrieve the small part of my suit I let melt away to lure people into a false sense of security. But for now, I needed a late-night snack.

Chapter 5

When you're a part of the "super" world, you have a few masks. It varies from person to person. Some use a literal mask with their other self, while others use their civilian identity as a metaphorical mask. I wiped my birth name from any sort of database years ago. Now there was only Malice. I could hide him behind a pair of glasses and a smile.

I kept several safe houses around the city, all under different names. I didn't stay at any of them for long, had to keep moving to avoid all the do-gooders, so buying groceries wasn't practical. Each safe house was based around a few different places I liked to eat at, places I could rotate through so I didn't become a regular and possibly be recognized. Right now it was about 1 AM, the witching hour. Since I kept odd hours, I typically chose places that stayed open late. The safe house closest to the cathedral, both of which would have to be scrapped after today's ordeal, was near a coffee shop that opened late and closed early in the morning. There were rarely more than a handful of people there, and this…this was probably the last time I'd get to go there for a while.

At the moment, there were a few people scattered around at the main bar. I flagged down the barista and ordered a dirty chai and a cheese danish. I skulked off with my items to a booth

15

in the corner, back turned to the majority. Thin tendrils of steam floated from my drink as I absentmindedly picked at my danish, my appetite fading as fatigue overtook me. The bell rang to signal another customer walking in. The low chatter of the cafe melded into white noise that dragged my eyelids closed, alongside each sip of my warm drink. Faux leather sighed behind me as someone took the booth right next to mine. Annoying for sure, but not worth causing a scene over.

My head jolted back as I fought off sleep, and suddenly warmth washed over me. It was comforting and pulled the weight of exhaustion off of me. My mood was better. Energy raced through my body. It inspired me, new plans forming at the back of my mind. And this presence felt…familiar. I grabbed the spoon from my drink and tapped it against the porcelain mug before sweeping it off my table. Metal clattered against tile, and I leaned over for my utensil. A spark passed between us as our fingers brushed against each other. I looked up into the amber eyes of Zarael, also hidden behind a pair of glasses. She seemed smaller out of her uniform. She had replaced her armor and tunic with a plain white tee and a black leather jacket. Her hair was blonde now and hung slightly curled around her head. A smile tugged at the corners of my lips as recognition flashed in her eyes. She beamed at me.

"Damn, those villain transports really suck. What do my tax dollars even go to?" She liked to joke that one of her powers was an infectious smile. Right now, I believed her.

"That's what you get for actually paying taxes."

She stood up and crossed her arms over her chest, one eyebrow cocked. "You don't pay taxes?"

I shrugged. "I don't think my income is technically taxable."

She rolled her eyes and went to sit back in her own booth. "I'll leave you be for now, since you're not actually doing anything, but watch your back tomorrow."

"Hey," I blurted out on a whim. "Why don't you join me?"

Her smile faltered.

"Not on 'The Dark Side' or anything. Just while you're here."

She looked around, as if anyone else here cared what she did. Finally, she grabbed her drink and sat opposite me. We sat in an awkward silence, both of us trying to think of something to talk about other than "work." She caved first.

"So, how'd you get out this time? Hidden lock pick? Fake seizure?"

I grinned and let my suit make me a new spoon, since I got the other one dirty. "New trick. The bit of my armor that makes up my cape is all that actually melted away. The rest stayed with me."

Zarael cringed at me. "Should you really be letting that thing touch your drink?"

I paused as I sucked the tea off the living metal spoon. "It's clean…I think."

I rushed to change the subject. "So, you got my origin story. What made Zarael, The Guardian Angel?"

Her smile fell completely this time. She looked around the room again, like someone was following her. "Well, okay. The official story, which I'm sure you've heard, is that I found this ancient armor on a trip to Egypt and used it to defend myself against some ancient automatons. That's a lie. I…grew up in a cult. The gold plate I wear is an artifact discovered by their founder when he was young. They passed it down until they believed we were in the last days. My brother was supposed to wear the armor, to be their holy warrior. But the night before he put it on, it called to me. It bound itself to me.

They…they tried to cut it off, but it didn't work. So I ran—well, flew—away. I didn't use the armor for years, but when more and more superheroes started popping up, I thought I could make a difference, power and responsibility and all that."

She understood. Here she stood, unbowed and unbroken, faced with such trauma. She was just like me. Impulse guided my hand to hers, and we locked eyes. She broke the silence first.

"Actually talking to you, it makes it seem like there's two versions you present to the world. Malice is just a performance you put on. But under all that hate and monologue, there's someone else. I just don't know his name."

That took me by surprise. I'd been Malice for so long, I hadn't even thought of my real name, let alone considered using it. "How about for now you can call me John. I'm a John Doe in the system, anyway."

She smiled at that. "All right then. And for now, you can call me Zee."

Hours passed like seconds. We stayed so long the barista started giving us dirty looks. So, we took our conversation outside. We stopped just outside the cafe, the dawn rushing up to meet us. I took her hand in mine.

"Can I see you again? Not for work, as Malice and Zarael. Like this, John and Zee."

She nodded. "Tomorrow? At the pier?"

"Sounds good."

By the time I got to the safe house, I was practically floating. As I drifted off to sleep, my dreams were tinged with gold.

Chapter 6

The next day I wandered the pier, waiting for Zarael. We hadn't exchanged numbers, so I had no way of knowing if she was on the way. I thought about doing a quick comb-through of the cathedral, see if there was anything usable, but that could wait. Anything important would've backed up and melted the evidence already.

It was a wonderfully gloomy day, gray storm clouds overhead set to burst at any moment. I leaned against the old wooden railing and looked out over the roiling ocean. My mind drifted to Zarael. In our late night and early morning encounters, I had memorized her face. She had a scar on her upper lip, whether from battle with me or not, I wasn't sure. And she smelled like oranges. Ripe on the tree. Just the warm comfort of her aura made me feel like anything was possible. Her words from the other night echoed in my mind. Maybe I could change. For her.

A prickle on the back of my neck brought me out of my thoughts. I ducked as two throwing knives embedded themselves in the wood before me. Behind me, Umbra melted out of the shadows. Their uniform was simpler than most heroes. They wore all black with armor that looked suspiciously like hockey pads. A dark mesh hung over their face and blurred any discernible features. It was rare to see them this far from Cion.

Strange, but not completely unheard of.

I spun around, my clothes already melting into armor. "What the hell? You use actual knives? No wonder you villains are fucking nuts."

Distracted, I barely noticed Thalassa claw her way out of the sea. I turned at her first hiss of oxygen. Her appearance was far more jarring than her companion. Her skin was the deathly blue of the recently drowned. Dead black eyes bore into me, unblinking. She kept her hands spread, thick webbing connecting the fingers. Thin black lines marked where gills hid in her abdomen. A mix of humanoid and aquatic features that struck fear into the common criminal. Kids loved her, for some reason. While Oceanus City was closer, having two extra heroes show up in the same city meant something was very wrong.

I had a hero on either side of me. I inched backwards, trying to get both of them in front of me. Energy arced around my fingertips, and I unleashed it in a flurry of arcing blasts, trying to maneuver the heroes closer together. As I raised both hands for a final massive shot, bolos propelled by an arrow wrapped around my wrists. I looked over and saw The Crimson Archer and his trick arrows had joined the fray. Fucking fantastic. He dressed in a bright red "archer" outfit, like someone would wear in a Robin Hood musical, complete with tights and a domino mask. He was stroking his stupid goatee like he'd actually done something impressive. If the city of New Nottingham's resident bleeding heart had made his way over here, Spire City itself may be in danger. He thumbed his stupid little hat up and looked skyward. I followed his gaze and froze. Zarael was floating in the air, flaming sword in hand.

Superheroes were a product of the modern age; less than one

hundred existed. Villains probably outnumbered them, but of course, no one could put aside their egos for those numbers to be used effectively. Heroes had no issue teaming up. Right now, most of The Pantheon, the premier hero group that inspired the others, had me surrounded. Which meant I had monumentally fucked up.

My mind raced, grasping for whatever it was I'd done to piss them off. Gordon was the son of someone important? One too many buildings blown up? Too many thoughts were flying, crashing together. Pressure built in my head until one thought remained. *Run.*

I snapped the bolos with a miniature arc of power and bolted. I threw my hands in front of me and chains flew out, reaching for the rooftops. But Zarael was there, faster than I'd ever seen her move before. She grabbed the chains and whipped them down, dragging me to my knees. Before I even had a chance to react, the ground disappeared from under me as Zarael pulled me into the air. A flick of the wrist sent me arcing over her, and another sent me straight back down.

I collided with the asphalt, the living metal just barely covering my head before impact, and the air was forced from my lungs. A gold plated boot slammed into my stomach, and my mask retracted so hot bile could spill out of my mouth. I rolled onto my back and gasped for air, black spots consuming my vision. As my eyes cleared, Zarael marched into view. Something was…off. She didn't have her usual aura. There was a slight glow, but it was more like a dim flashlight instead of a warm flame. Her eyes had faded to a sickly yellow. Dark circles had formed beneath them. Her skin was extremely pale. I could practically see the veins underneath. I saw clearly then. There was no comforting presence, no scent of oranges, not even her scar. The storm finally broke as everything clicked together. The sole explanation.

"You're not her."

The False Angel glared at me.

I looked around at the other heroes. "Are you all stupid? Look at her! That's not the real Zarael."

The others looked at each other, but the imposter never changed her gaze. Thalassa signed, "He's lost it." Umbra nodded in agreement.

"What? My escape is so important, you're that blinded to what's in front of you?"

The fake Zarael scowled at me. "You take priority, murderer."

I rolled my eyes. "Oh, come on! Gordon was dealing to kids. Surely, you could look the other way on this one. Or is his daddy really that important?"

Anger, or something close to it, flashed across her face. "Maybe you really have lost it."

I looked around at the assembled heroes again, searching for any kind of answer. I swear a smile played across her lips, disappearing before the other heroes took notice.

"We're here because you killed the driver and the man guarding you during your escape. Curtis, I think his name was."

More vomit threatened to push its way out as the world spun around me. "No…"

A fake tear slid down The False Angel's cheek. "Monster, you don't even remember."

I slammed my fists on the ground, launching myself upright. The living metal reacted to my anger, transforming into a writhing mass of weaponry. Blades burst from my back, cannons formed around my hands. Spider-like limbs stretched out from my sides.

"Lies! I didn't kill him; you did!"

Before a single attack could connect, The False Angel grabbed my chest plate and pulled. The living metal stretched but refused to leave me. As I angled my weapons at her, Zarael unleashed a torrent of harsh light that burned through every single drop of my living metal. She dropped me back on the ground, my skin burnt and smoking in a few scattered batches. Then, the world turned black.

Chapter 7

I woke up in a straitjacket.

They left me curled up on the floor of a cell, not my usual one either. It was incredibly narrow. There was a toilet built into the floor that was maybe two feet away. There was no bed, just cracked stone floor. It was cold and damp. Actually, damp didn't cover it. The cell was completely drenched, with water collecting in the corners and pooling on the floor. Moss, or maybe even mold, grew in rough patches all over the walls. A lantern hung from the ceiling, making the shadows dance across the walls. The smell of rot permeated the air. I struggled to sit up, but the straitjacket did its job. A hand grabbed me and pulled me into the air. I stared into the putrid yellow eyes of The False Angel.

She scowled at me. "Pathetic."

The imposter threw me into the back of the cell, slamming me against the wall. I landed on one knee, the impact numbing my leg. I launched myself with my other leg, charging at the fake Zarael. The rattle of a chain and a pull at my back stopped me halfway up the cell. I thrashed against the chain, near feral, before dropping to my knees. My voice came out in a pained growl.

"Who are you?"

She smiled and spread her wings, blocking the cell door. "Guess you got hit harder than we thought. I'm the Guardian Angel of Spire City and, for now, your warden."

I glared at her behind a curtain of hair. "Where am I?"

Zarael laughed, a cold thing devoid of any emotion. "Curtis was a good guy, had a lot of friends. No one who had any qualms about me burying you. Even the 'proper' authorities are looking the other way. So honestly, the where doesn't matter. You'll die here."

She turned to leave. "Someone will probably drop off some food, but don't hold your breath. Or do, then we don't have to waste the resources."

"Wait!"

She stopped in the doorway, not bothering to look at me.

"Did you mean any of what you said the other day?"

Now she turned, a wicked smile on her face. "No. I just needed you out in the open."

The ancient cell door slammed behind her, adding new cracks to the wall. Laughter echoed throughout my prison.

***

I sat in the near dark, shadows writhing around me. I couldn't tell how much time had passed or if it was passing at all. Maybe time had simply stopped. As the water dripped from the ceiling in a steady beat, I found myself drowning in despair. It hurt to think of the loss of Zarael, of my chance to change for her. Maybe even be with her. The pain of what could have been weighed on me like a crown of thorns. As I lay on the wet stone, my thoughts drifted to Curtis. Curtis was kind, was a good man. He didn't deserve to be "was." He should be home with his daughter. But he wasn't, and that was my fault.

No. The False Angel did this.

Rage boiled over inside of me. What was the point in changing for a world that let someone like Curtis die? No, I was a villain. Now it was time to fucking act like it.

I pushed myself back up and clambered to my feet. The straitjacket was first. I could feel the cold air stabbing through tears in the cloth. It was already weak. I just needed to apply pressure. Something quick and sharp. I ran as fast as the space would allow me. The chain jerked; the sudden stop and wet floor made for a poor combination. My feet slid out from under me, and gravity put me back on the floor. Something ripped. Maybe the jacket, probably muscle.

Alternative approach. I leaned forward, pulling against the chain. I pushed one foot down, letting it slide before planting the next one, constantly stretching the fabric against the metal. I jerked forward once, twice, and finally flew forward. I rolled over onto my back. Behind me was the chain, the end now only holding a ragged piece of gray cloth. Not a lot, but enough for me to get out. I pushed the jacket forward, freeing my neck. I wiggled my arms out with some effort. The rest of it slid off my legs, and I was free.

Now I needed a weapon, just in case The False Angel was still here. The rusty chain I was just connected to would have to do. Hopefully, time had made it weak enough for me to remove it. I wrapped both hands around the base of the chain and pulled. Metal ground against metal, but the chain held fast. I moved back a few steps, placing my hands farther down the chain, hoping to find a weaker link. I leaned forward, then pulled back as hard as I could. My hands stung as the old metal bit into my palms, tearing the skin open. I let out a cry of pain and frustration. I hated this. Hated being stuck, being hurt. I could use that hate. I grabbed the chain again, wrapping it around my hands this time. The sound of the chain grinding against itself echoed in my ears as I pulled it, driven by the pain and hate. I let the chain go slack and practically jumped backwards, screaming into the dark as I went. The chain snapped back, free from its mount. Red lines of irritation marred my hands as I marched towards the door, ready to face my warden.

I stopped just before I touched the cold metal handle. I could hear something moving down the hall. Footsteps scraped across the stone floor, slowing to a halt just outside my door. A ragged sound, breathing maybe, echoed in front of my cell. I wasn't alone.

Chapter 8

The air froze in my lungs.

This wasn't The False Angel. Whatever was on the other side of the door was scratching like an animal, frantically trying to get in. Something clicked and the door opened just a crack, letting in the nauseatingly sweet smell of burnt flesh. Blackened fingers pushed themselves through the opening, grasping the door. I sidestepped behind the door as it swung inward, hoping the creaking whine it made hid the sound of the chain. The intruder stood in the doorway, hidden by the same slab of metal that protected me from it. After what seemed like an eternity, it lost interest. My lungs burned as the footsteps scraped away, back down the hall. When I finally felt it was safe, I gasped and sucked in a deep breath. The footsteps, far but not far enough, stopped again. Every muscle in my body clenched, desperately waiting for them to move on. Once they had gone, I felt my legs trembling as I forced myself to move away from the door.

I made my way out into the hallway. The corridor was lined with identical doors, spread out farther than the cramped rooms needed. A solitary confinement wing then. Flickering caged lights attempted to illuminate the way but really only created an epileptic's nightmare. The hallway opened up to a round room with a coiled stone staircase in the center and six more identical passageways leading off from it. Water spilled down the steps, and I could hear the rain still going up above. I was almost to the stairs when the lights finally died, stranding me in darkness. As if on cue, the scraping footsteps returned, echoing out from the corridor right across from the one I had just left. I bolted towards the stairs. I had a rusty chain and absolutely no desire to see what was down here.

The staircase coiled its way up, leading to a large circular room above. Rusted metal bars lined unfinished walls, open to the elements. At the core of the area was a watchtower, with a sharp beam of light emitting from it, illuminating the empty cells as it circled the room. I realized exactly where I was. Nove Cerchi. An old-style penitentiary, as in strict discipline bordering on torture. Founded by an overtly religious asshole with too much money, Nove Cerchi sat on an island in the bay so all the undesirables were kept far from sparkling Spire City. But it turned out shipping materials to the island was more trouble than it was worth. A few particularly nasty storms even took out some of the boats transporting supplies. In the end, Nove Cerchi's benefactor sunk all his money into a prison that was never finished and died penniless. Very sad, I know. But even with no ghosts, something lingered.

I circled around the base of the watchtower, looking for a way in. If I got high enough, I could get my bearings, see if there was a dock or a boathouse. I could even try to get the light to pulse out an SOS. On the other side of the tower's base was a metal door ripped from its hinges. The other had already been through here. Another set of stairs wound into the tower. Maybe even to salvation. I went to run up the steps, but before my foot even landed on the third one, a hand grabbed me by the throat and tore me back outside. I slid across the wet stone as I was finally confronted by what followed behind.

Unnatural, tumorous, red muscle burst through broken seams in the burnt skin. Bone-tipped claws twitched at the ends of uneven arms. The creature hunched over from the weight of a second torso fused to its back. The arms of the other body had been stretched to thin, the muscle and skin barely enough to cover the gray bone, and the ends had been transformed into sharp bone spears. Two skulls melted into each other with what little flesh they had left. Their lipless mouths hung open, black tongues panting in tandem. One eye in each face had been turned into an obsidian orb with the sickly yellow pupils of The False Angel. The others just lolled, unfocused, in their sockets. All it wore was a pair of broken boots and a pair of tattered gray pants. Clipped to the waistband were two IDs, their edges tinged with blackened plastic. They were left there to taunt me, to show me the creature had a name. Had once been someone I knew.

Curtis.

Chapter 9

"Curtis..."

He stopped, both of his eyes focusing like they recognized me. I took a step forward, desperately searching for whatever spark of him remained. As I drew near, one of the bone spears flew out, slicing into my shoulder. I stumbled back and pressed my hand to the wound as the blood slowly seeped down my arm. Curtis studied the sanguine fluid on his extra limb. With his thumb, he wiped away the blood from the bone blade and then licked it off, leaving a scarlet trail on his tongue that he seemed to savor. There was a glint in those onyx eyes that echoed the fake Zarael.

"What did she do to you?"

That seemed to stop him. His dirty teeth cracked open and his twin mouths let out the most horrific scream I'd ever heard in my life. Curtis was gone. My friend was dead. Whatever grotesque corpse he had left behind was just a puppet for The False Angel.

I tightened my grip on the chain, trying to bring it up, lash out with it. But I couldn't. Even if it was just a shell of the person I'd known, I couldn't bring my anger to bear against him. So, I spun around and ran. I had noticed a possible exit when I'd gotten around the watchtower. Another set of stairs ran straight out of the circular part. Angled up, I assumed, so prisoners and guards could climb to a metaphorical heaven. I bolted up the stairs, given only brief flashes of where I was going from the tower's rotating light.

A thunderous pulse replaced the heavy scrape of boots on stone as Curtis dropped to all fours and rushed after me. I struggled to stay upright and tripped over every other step. My last attempt dropped me in front of a hallway immersed in a darkness that not even the watchtower could reach. I rolled onto my back, assuming Curtis would come crashing down on top of me. My breathing was the only sound that pierced the silence as I glanced around. The watchtower made its loop, and I noticed that Curtis's boots had finally broken apart and were left abandoned on the ground. Curtis himself was nowhere to be seen.

I steadied myself against the wall, desperate to regain my breath. My legs felt like they were on fire after the sudden and brief exertion. I wandered down the hallway, my eyes desperately searching for any sign of my pursuer. As I slowly adjusted to the darkness, I caught my reflection in the window. My eyes had become hollow, and dark purple circles had appeared around them. My shoulder had stopped bleeding, and sticky residue left marks on my arm. The world beyond my reflection was dark. All I could see through the window was rain beating against the pane. I squinted my eyes as if doing so would grant me night vision. The hall seemed to go on forever. This whole place was strange. The main area had some electricity, but that didn't extend to this hall or the cells. Maybe this place was more madness than method.

Lost in thought, I didn't see the massive hand slam through the window. Shards of glass and rainfall crashed inward, jarring me out of my trance. Curtis ripped me from the hall, sending me flying into the rain. I slid through mud and tore through overgrown foliage. I felt the sharp sting of cuts opening up on my arms and legs. Curtis crouched on the roof, his gaze fixed on me. He—it—wanted me to run. It wanted a hunt.

Fine. I'd give it a hunt.

I pushed myself to my feet and launched forward, stumbling into the forest. Nature had reclaimed the island. Anything beyond the penitentiary was lush and green. After I had gone a few steps, I spun around at the sound of a branch cracking to find that Curtis was no longer in sight. I didn't run. I wasn't about to die tired. The surrounding trees shook in the storm, swaying like they were trying to block out the sky. I had no idea where I was or where I was heading. If I could keep moving in a straight line, I should find some sort of shelter. Maybe.

Even though I couldn't make him out, I could tell Curtis was in the trees. Every time I heard a snapping tree branch or rustling in the brush, I knew it was him. It was all intentional, all an attempt to get in my head. I could see shards of bark flying from the shadows now and then, reminding me he was there. He was trying to herd me. I ignored his prompts, choosing to keep blazing forward.

Green gave way to black. The terrain sloped downwards slightly, forming a small crater. At its center was a corpse. Judging from the uniform, it was a hero's body. One of the space-based Pantheon members. The chest had exploded outward, forming a cave of broken ribs. Emerald shards, probably their power source, glittered around it. Their face had been crushed in, the skin burnt and disfigured. The body was already bloated and stiff. Curtis didn't do this. That same twin scream rang out again, echoing all around me, hiding its source.

I spun around and searched for any sign of Curtis. I surveyed the area, feeling the hair on the back of my neck rise in anticipation. As I stepped back, I heard his heavy breathing right behind me. I tried to run away, but one heavy hand smacked me to the ground. Blood and dirt mixed in my mouth. Curtis wrenched me upright and put us eye to eye. I spat the grimy wad into one of his faces. He sent me flying across the crater in return, slamming into its edge. As I struggled to regain my breath, pain gripped my right hand. Looking down, I saw the rusty chain wrapped around my hand, bruising and cutting the skin.

If I kept dwelling on the fact that this was Curtis, I was going to die. I focused on the pain and dredged up every ounce of anger I had left. I let him approach, and as he loomed over me, ready to kill, I lashed out. My rusty chain connected with bone, barely knocking away a bone spear aimed at my chest. A few sharp bone fragments scattered around me, breaking from the spot where I had struck. Now there was an opening. I just needed to apply pressure.

I managed to roll onto my feet, barely keeping my balance, and pushed my advantage. Metal and bone collided as I struck with the chain again. All my attention was focused on one spear. I barely noticed the second one coming towards me. I narrowly dodged it, quickly lashing out with the chain in retaliation. Because of my mistake, several rusty links were sent flying off in the counterattack.

Curtis followed up with the weakened spear, cutting into my leg and embedding itself into the ground. The chain slipped from my hand as I muffled a cry of pain. I slammed my hand against the crack in the spear. It bent from the impact, but not enough to break it away completely.

I kept up my barrage until a part of the spear snapped off. Curtis screamed and slammed a fist into my stomach, sending me flying into the air. I got back up faster this time, running and claiming my prize. The broken spear tip emerged from the ground with minimal effort. I took my new weapon and sprinted at Curtis, stabbing it through his abdomen. I kept pushing and pressing him until I finally forced him to the ground. He slid and landed on his back, the spear going through him and into the sucking mud. The other spear came flying towards me, and I managed to catch it, using my rage to bend it back until it ultimately snapped off. The pain it caused Curtis earned me a back-handed slap, sending me rolling through the mud.

That was fine. It put me closer to where I wanted to be. I found the chain in the mud and wrapped it back around my hand. Curtis watched as I approached him, pinned by his own spear. I took a long, hard look at him, really studying him. This pathetic monstrosity didn't deserve to wear his face. I slammed the chain down with a satisfying crack, the skin between the two heads ripping apart.

It screamed as I brought the chain down again and again. Blood and rusted metal flew through the air. Eventually, it stopped and just stared at me with empty eyes. I didn't stop my assault until its head was a bloody smear on the ground, chain links littered around it. I stood panting in the rain, my face covered in sweat and gore.

Chapter 10

I stumbled through the forest, silently pleading with it to release me. After a long while of shambling through twisting paths and dead ends, the green gave way to an empty beach.

The rain had stopped, but dark clouds still hung heavy in the air. An ancient dock clung to the sand, the rotting wood collapsing into the sea. Of course, after decades of neglect, why would there be a boat here? I scanned the shoreline for any sign of a boat that might notice me. Nothing. I was stranded like a rat left on a rock in the ocean, silently screaming for salvation.

There was no use wallowing in self-pity. I ambled along the beach, looking for anything that might help me off this godforsaken rock. My search led me to the bottom of a cliff, just below the ruins of Nove Cerchi. Hope came in the form of a ramshackle cabin and boathouse. Probably for the groundskeeper or whoever they were going to have live on site. Nothing on this stupid island made sense. The cabin had mostly fallen apart. The door hung at an angle in its frame. Half of the roof had collapsed, and the windows were all in odd shapes.

I raided the cabin first. I stumbled upon a first aid kit in my first stroke of luck. The metal container had preserved its contents. The elements destroyed the rest of the cabin, so I bandaged my wounds and moved on. My luck held with the boathouse.

It was in much better shape; only a few places on the roof had been punctured. Inside, the wood was warped and rotten. I had to choose my steps carefully. The boat that was housed here was small, the motor slightly rusted, but the blades could still spin. I found a can of fuel and dumped what was left into the engine, hoping it was more gas than water. A cabinet in the boathouse yielded some flares. The boat probably wouldn't get me all the way to the city. I'd have to take my chances with whoever was out on the water. I dumped my findings into the boat and pushed the double doors open. A combination of rusted hinges and rotten wood caused them to fall into the ocean once they'd fully opened. No surprise there. I braced my shoulder against the front of the boat and pushed, the wood grinding against the ramp. I leapt into the boat and, after a few false starts, got the motor running. The water churned behind me as I aimed the boat towards city lights.

The boat cut through the black water, bouncing with each wave. Alone in the darkness with nothing to direct my rage at, the fire inside dwindled. Any adrenaline I had left faded. Without either of them, I was just tired and empty. My eyelids grew heavy, my breathing slowed. My grip on the motor's handle loosened as my head nodded forward. Fatigue was dragging me into sleep.

Something slammed into the boat, and sleep lost its hold on me. Another blow sent the boat fishtailing. The motor put up a fight as it struggled to find purchase in the water. A third blow carved into the side of the boat, sending black water pouring in, and something slithered out. A final jolt killed the ancient motor, stranding me in the dark. As I ignited one of the flares, a bright red circle of light formed around me and banished the darkness. The water stilled as I swung my flare in the night, searching for any sign of help. I couldn't shake the feeling that I was being watched from beneath the surface. Peering into the inky black water, I could just make out a shape writhing in the dark.

A white light flared up behind me. The water churned around me, and a roar filled the air. An inhuman sound. It turned in the water, sending a wave towards me and spilling more water into my boat.

"Well, what have we here?"

A portly man stood on the bow of the Coast Guard boat, hands firmly placed on his hips. A stocky, slightly shorter man aimed the search light behind him.

"Loonie out the asylum, Skipper," the other man replied, his voice higher pitched than his commanding officer's with a slight British accent. "I didn't think we had one of those out here."

"That we do not, Mr. Knights. That we do not." He spoke at varying levels of intensity, seemingly unaware of how his voice changed.

A tall, gaunt man silently approached from behind the other two. He studied me from behind a pair of round, rimless glasses. "Sir, I believe that is the supervillain, Malice, recently apprehended by Zarael. Currently, he is sinking."

"Astute observation, Mr. Miller. Guess we better bring that scum aboard so we can re-apprehend him." The captain pointed at me with his entire hand, all four fingers aimed at me. "Mr. DiMaggio, bring that scum aboard."

A large hand gripped the back of my shirt and yanked me from my boat, dropping me onto the deck of the Coast Guard ship. I stared up into the face of the six-and-a-half-foot-tall ginger man who loomed over me, scars crisscrossing his pale skin. The other three joined and formed a circle around me.

"Isn't this a sorry sight?" said the captain.

He was right. My clothes were completely soaked through and clung tight to my skin. The rain had carved lines into the mud that covered me, unable to wash it all the way off. I couldn't tell if they could see the red streaking down my face.

"Now, how'd you get out of prison, criminal?"

I struggled to my feet, my legs suddenly sore and uncooperative. "Wasn't too difficult, considering Zarael didn't take me there. She threw me in Nove Cerchi and had some mutated corpse guarding me."

The captain looked me up and down, clearly skeptical. "Uh-huh. And why would she do that?"

The fire flared back inside me. "Zarael's been replaced. By an alien, clone, multiversal doppelgänger, I don't know. Whatever it is has it out for me. Obviously, I came from somewhere close. That piece of shit clearly would not get far." I gestured to the little motor boat as its stern slid into the water, tossing a few pitiful bubbles up behind it.

Without breaking eye contact, the captain addressed his men. "Mr. Miller, any information on a fake Zarael running around?"

"No, Skipper."

"Hmm." The captain turned and walked towards the cockpit, hands clasped behind his back. "Mr. DiMaggio, get this criminal in cuffs."

The large man nodded and skulked off towards the rear of the boat. The other two dispersed, Miller following the captain while Knights returned to his spotlight and smiled at me with empty eyes. There wasn't any point in running, or swimming, really. Might as well wait for Lurch to return and stow me wherever the Coast Guard put their catch of the day. Probably on an inner tube tied to the boat with a rope, hoping their quarry wouldn't get thrown off.

Odd that they just happened to come across me. It didn't even seem like they knew I was out here. The "proper" authorities must've really trusted the fake Zarael to keep me on the island. Or she hadn't actually talked to them. But someone in The Pantheon should've said something. Or it was entirely possible they just didn't loop The Coast Guard in to supervillain affairs.

The boat jerked down suddenly and pulled me out of my thoughts. Irritation flashed through me. What was taking the ginger giant so long? I could've gotten my own handcuffs by now. Judging from Smiley, the four of them probably shared a brain cell, and Slenderman held on to it tight.

Speaking of, Mr. Knights didn't seem particularly interested in what I was doing. I did a very nonchalant stretch and took off to find the largest of my captors. Since the boat wasn't moving yet, I was assuming they were waiting for him to lock me up. It wasn't that big of a ship; he couldn't have gotten lost.

I made my way past the cockpit. A quick glance inside showed the captain and Miller struggling with the controls. Of course they'd have problems with their own boat. Rounding the corner revealed part of the railing had been ripped off, something the captain should've noticed. DiMaggio was hunched over in the corner, rivulets of water streaming off his body. Probably fell in with the railing. As I got closer, I noticed a horrific wet sucking sound. It looked like there were cuts on either side of DiMaggio's torso. They moved in tandem with the sound. The smell of dead fish grew with each wet rasp. Looking closer, I realized they weren't cuts, but gills. Thalassa rose and turned to face me, clutching DiMaggio close as she consumed him.

Chapter 11

Thalassa had been ripped apart and put back together by someone with very limited knowledge of marine biology.

Just like Curtis, tumorous muscle had increased her height and build. Her gills were unmistakably larger, deep ridges with ragged edges instead of thin lines, shrinking and expanding as they sucked in air. Her left arm had been replaced with a lobster's claw, and rough chitin covered purple muscle that threatened to bulge out with every movement. The claw itself was carefully honed and sharpened so that it had cutting edges and razor points, transforming its use from crushing to tearing. Her other arm split into five tentacles at what used to be an elbow, suckers lined with curved teeth. Each tentacle had ensnared one of DiMaggio's limbs. Blood dripped from where teeth bit into flesh. DiMaggio's body was slowly being fed into the star-shaped pattern on her chest filled with writhing tendrils, each one clamoring to grab hold of him. Digestive fluid spilled off the stump where his head had been. A dark, gaping hole filled with an array of twitching teeth that glimmered in the light marked the place where Thalassa's mouth should be.

Thalassa studied me with a pair of bulbous black eyes that protruded from her skull. Something clicked in her brain and she slipped back into the water, dragging away what was left of DiMaggio's body. I stepped backwards, careful not to let my gaze drift from the damaged corner of the ship. After several agonizing seconds, my hand found the cold metal shell of the cockpit. My fingers scratched against the metal, vehemently grasping for the door handle. Then the world fell away.

I knocked the captain back into the cockpit as I tumbled backwards.

"What the hell is this? Are you still not in cuffs?"

I righted myself and turned to face him. "We need to get out of here. Now."

The captain scowled at me. "We're working on it, convict. Where's DiMaggio?"

Outright telling him one of their heroes had eaten his head probably wouldn't be beneficial. "There's something in the water. I don't know what, but it was eating him."

The captain just narrowed his eyes at me. "Sure. Monster in the water. Miller, get the prisoner locked up. DiMaggio probably got knocked overboard. I'll go toss him a line."

He shoved past me, not even acknowledging the damage to his ship. I trailed behind him, trying to get him to listen. Miller was too engrossed in fixing the boat to try to stop me.

"Captain, we have to get out of here. This creature is after me, and I don't think it wants any witnesses."

"Interesting theory. You wanna back it up with some facts?"

"Yeah, let me just go ask it."

"Have fun with that."

I could feel my teeth grinding into dust. This man was insufferable. I didn't even know why I was trying. He and his entire crew could plunge into the depths with Thalassa for all I cared. Then again, they could've just left me to sink and didn't. That might count for something. The captain pulled a life preserver ring from the side railing and stomped off to where he believed DiMaggio had gone overboard. Knights's empty stare drifted over to me, one eye lagging behind the other.

"Don't mind the skipper. He's hardheaded, but he means well." He smiled, a cheesy-looking thing with far too many teeth. But sincere. Like Curtis. Maybe there were enough people like him. People worth saving, worth being something else for.

I felt a smile tug at the corner of my mouth. Maybe there was a better way to get the captain to listen, and fast. I turned to go find him just as he marched back up to where I was, his face a bright scarlet.

"What the hell happened to my ship?"

Thalassa's tentacles burst from the dark water and wrapped around the front railing of the ship. The ship's bow dipped underwater as she pulled herself onto the deck. Gravity wrenched us towards her, then threw us to the ground as the boat righted itself. Knights scrambled across the deck, repeatedly trying and failing to get on his feet. Unfortunately, with a ship this small, he was stuck in her path. A webbed foot came crashing down onto his back with a sickening crunch, reverberating beneath it. The next step landed on his hand, splaying his fingers at odd and painful angles. Thalassa's gaze briefly wavered from me, finally realizing something was trapped beneath her feet. She looked down at her hostage, then back at me and the captain. Tears swam in Knights's eyes as Thalassa placed a foot on his head.

"Skipper..."

His head cracked open as Thalassa pushed down. Gore and brain matter burst across the deck like overripe fruit. Knights's eyes rolled around on the floor. Thalassa bent and delicately picked one up in her claw, popping it into the nightmare hole that made up her mouth. Vitreous dripped down her front as the eye cracked open. Something almost like purring echoed in her throat.

The color drained from the captain's face, his expression frozen in shock. Then, scarlet rage colored his skin as he charged at the altered former hero. She had taken two people dear to him. She was now the target of his righteous fury. But to Thalassa, he was nothing. All it took was a swipe from her claw, and the captain went flying, blood streaming after him. He nearly cleared the cockpit, but hit the roof at the last second, tossing him into a spiral. His head struck the railing, and he sank into the water.

I scrambled back, desperate for any kind of weapon. Thalassa followed, the boat angling to the side under her weight. I nearly threw myself around the corner trying to get to Miller. My fingers slid underneath the latch and snapped it back. Nothing. I looked into the window and stared at Miller. He just stood, back to the controls, and shook his head. I struck my fist against the window in frustration, releasing an angry cry of disappointment. I didn't have time to be angry. Pushing off the metal door, I ran to the other side of the boat, hoping that there was another life preserver ring I could use and, I don't know, fucking paddle it to shore?

Unfortunately for Miller, Thalassa didn't have the patience to go around. Her claw sent glass flying into the cockpit, then arced back and tore through the metal. Another slash cut down, clearing a path she could walk through. Miller cowered in the corner, too afraid to fight for his own life. I watched as Thalassa's tentacles snaked into the cockpit and grabbed hold of Miller. Guts and gore spewed out of him as she drove her claw through his torso. She tossed the body through the frontmost window, discarding it like an empty banana peel. Miller lay dead and broken across the useless wheel. Among all the red dripping onto the floor, something stood out. I had one shot. I waited as Thalassa ducked into the cockpit, waited until she drew back that monstrous claw to smash open the last window. I stepped back, my hands making sure there was no railing behind me. Then, I jumped.

The cold water stunned me, costing me valuable time. This was her domain. I couldn't afford to be down here for long. I pushed forward as the muffled sound of breaking glass exploded over the water. My hands guided me along the bottom of the boat, desperately searching for the edge. Thalassa dropped down into the water, letting herself sink as her tentacles spread out, reaching after me.

I pulled myself out from under the boat and broke the surface of the water. I threw an arm over the edge of the boat and pulled myself back up as fast as my tired muscles would let me. Thalassa's tentacles were already snaking out of the water, wrapping themselves around anything they could. A dull thunk reverberated through the deck as she pierced the underside of the boat with her claw.

I dove into the shattered remains of the cockpit, scrambling across the floor for what I needed. My vision blurred as saltwater leaked into my eyes, stinging with each drop. My fingers wrapped around the gun's grip just as Thalassa pulled herself back up, the sudden weight shaking my balance and throwing me onto my back. I clasped both hands around the gun and did my best to aim upside down through a film of seawater. Thalassa's blurry form loomed into view, and I pulled the trigger. A fireball shot out and lodged itself into the fallen hero's flesh. Just a flare gun, fucking typical.

Thalassa screamed in pain regardless, a horrible screeching sound that cut into my ears. She stumbled back as her tentacles flailed wildly in the air. I needed something, anything, to finish her. Fortunately, she'd given me what I needed. I grabbed the biggest shard of glass I could find and rushed to her. Black blood squirted into the air as the glass dug into her neck. She fell back into the water, my momentum taking me with her. Thalassa splashed into the water with a painful slap. I turned to climb back onto the boat, for all the good it would do me, but one of her tentacles found my leg, and the others quickly followed after. She sank into the freezing water, intent on taking me to death's door with her.

The fires of my rage flared up. I didn't survive all that just to die with her. If we were both going to die, I was going to make damn sure she went first. I swam straight at her, latching on to her skull with both hands. I drove my thumbs into her bulging eyes, feeling a satisfying scrunch as I blinded her. Another scream echoed through the water. I needed her to die afraid, in the dark. I kept pushing and pushing, keeping her head centered between my hands. My lungs were burning, but I kept squeezing and squeezing. Everything I had left went into killing her. I felt something crack beneath my hands as I faded into black.

Chapter 12

I was lost, floating aimlessly in the darkness. I could feel something beneath me. It felt like I was on my stomach. Or no, I was hanging off of something. Cold washed over me, the world rose and fell around me. The cold took me higher, and I was flying. Whatever I was hanging on to fell away and I fell with it.

The cold grabbed me and slammed me into something solid. Air rushed from my lungs, and I woke up gasping. I caught a single breath of air before my stomach convulsed, shooting salt water up into my mouth. Vomit poured out of me as I flipped over onto my hands and knees. The ground sank beneath my palms. Sand. I was on a beach, icy water encircling me. I made it back. Behind me floated my salvation.

The captain's arm was caught in the rope handles of an orange life preserver. The rest of him lay face down in the water, thin red lines floating in the black waves. He saved me. He saved me and I didn't even know his name. I forced myself to my feet and waded into the sea. He was ice cold. No life had pumped through him for a while. I lugged his body to the beach and placed him down gently on his back. A ragged gash carved across his torso, another hung across his forehead just above his eyes. I searched his body, desperate for any identification.

His dog tags clinked against themselves as I pulled them from under his ruined uniform. Skipper McGrath.

Metal bit into my palm as I grasped the tags in my hand. I didn't know if this world deserved to be saved. Hell, I didn't even know if this city deserved salvation. But those who died because of The False Angel, because of me, deserved vengeance.

She took Zarael.

She took Curtis.

She took McGrath, Knights, Miller, and DiMaggio.

She could have left well enough alone, been just another villain. But no. It was one thing to go after me. It was another to hurt those who helped me despite what I was. For her transgressions, The False Angel would burn.

I marched across the beach, steadfast in my mission. I needed the scraps of my living metal, needed to make her pay. Splinters dug into my already damaged palms as I clambered up the boardwalk. I didn't have the patience to find an easier way out. I slid under the wooden railing and observed my surroundings. Pain wracked my body before I could find anything of note. My limbs hung heavy at my sides. My stomach was a whining hole of hunger. I needed food, needed caffeine. Maybe some painkillers.

I shambled across the silent streets. Each step had become a herculean task. A group of kids on bikes shot down the asphalt, disappearing into the darkness behind me. I barely registered the metal suddenly clattering against the road, chalking it up to a series of sudden dismounts. As I rounded the corner, the world darkened. I froze, unable to move in anticipation of Zarael's next attack. But the darkness faded, revealing the light of my saving grace. My contacts had reacted to the neon signage of a 24-hour convenience store.

Cold air beckoned me forward as the automatic doors opened. Harsh white light illuminated the space, exposing any sort of grime that covered the floor. Numb legs carried me into the store, and a squelching noise filled the store as I left a trail of wet sand behind me. The teenage cashier, his face red and angry with acne, just watched as I made my way through the store, not paid enough to care. Glazed-over eyes followed me as I ripped open the door to the energy drinks. I let the cold air shock me back to life before chugging and crushing a whole can. The bent aluminum clattered to the floor as I reached in for a second can. I looked back at the cashier, and his eyes widened in recognition.

"HOLY FUCKING SHIT! You're Malice!" he announced to the entirety of Spire City, voice squeaking with excitement.

I just shrugged and gave him a quick smile. "I get that sometimes. It's the hair."

The kid just about ran out from behind the counter. "Nah, man. I know it's you. I'm a massive fucking fan. I'd know you anywhere. Hey, check this out."

He pulled up his shirt sleeve to show off a crude tattoo of me, fully suited up, my arms crossed over my chest with a sickle in each hand. A black banner read "WE LIVE IN A SOCIETY" in the twisting scratched-up font of a black metal band. The skin around the tattoo was bright red and clearly irritated. It was either fresh or infected.

My face painfully contorted into an awkward smile. "Oh, wow. That's…really something." I glanced down at the crushed can on the floor. "Uh, full disclosure. I can't pay for these."

The kid laughed. Again, way too loud. "Malice? THE Lord of Dread? Paying for this shit? No fucking way, man. You're an agent of chaos, trying to tear down this society that keeps the free thinkers down! A society that feeds us poison, so we buy their cures while they suppress our medicine."

Jesus Christ, do I actually sound like that?

"M'lord. This…is on the house."

I shot him another awkward smile. "Oh, cool…dude." I looked behind him, a tray of fried chicken tenders enticing me from behind curved plastic. "Maybe some of those, too?"

***

The cold air followed me out, flowing into the night. I cracked open another energy drink. The cashier had filled an entire bag for me while I ravenously scarfed down more than enough chicken. Caffeinated and fed, my mind wandered. That kid had called me an agent of chaos. It gave the impression that my actions held no purpose and that I was simply destroying for the sake of destruction. But my actions had a cause. A just cause, in fact. Or, I thought they did.

I felt a chill run down my spine as the tiny hairs on the back of my neck stood up. I looked around, suddenly noticing it was oppressively dark now. The streetlights were emitting a dim, barely visible glimmer of sickly yellow light. As I raised the can to my lips, it spun away, impaled on a throwing knife. I let out a heavy sigh and slowly turned to face the shadows across the street. I stood and waited for Umbra to make their way out of the darkness, yet no one appeared.

"Hello?"

Nothing.

"If it's alright with you, I really don't feel like doing this."

Again, nothing. I squinted and tried to make out any kind of shape in the darkness. I swear I could see something standing there.

Something struck me square in the face, sending blood spurting from both nostrils. The blow was padded, not just someone's fist. I clasped a hand to my nose and watched as one of Crimson Archer's boxing glove arrows rolled across the sidewalk.

"Stop right there, evil doer!"

Well, looked like not even The False Angel could make use of Crimson Archer. No surprise there. Another arrow launched from the adjacent rooftop, wrapping a cable around a light pole. Archer zip lined down and rolled as he hit the ground, popping back up and nocking another arrow, pointed right at me.

"I'm stopped!" Cautiously, I pinched my nose, and a throbbing sensation radiated up to my brain. "I think you broke my nose. Fucking prick."

"Your tricks won't work on me, evil doer!"

Jesus Christ.

"Don't you have something better to do? Isn't Thalassa missing or something?"

That got to him. He lowered his bow, concern leaking into his face.

"No, not that I know of." Anger flashed in his eyes as he aimed back at me. "Why? What did you do?"

"Nothing! That Fake Zarael mutated her and left her guarding the bay in case I left Nove Cerchi."

The fucker rolled his eyes at me. "This again? No one replaced Zarael. She's completely fine. But what were you doing at Nove Cerchi?"

"Fucking what? That's where you all left me." I gestured to my current messy look. "Look at me! Does it look like I came from the prison?"

He scowled. "Of course not. You escaped from Zarael's custody. We've been looking for you ever since."

Of course that's what happened. They probably paired off, too. That's how The False Angel got Thalassa alone long enough to change her. I pinched the bridge of my nose in anger, causing my face to hurt more.

"Where did Umbra go? They have a fucking brain cell to comprehend all this."

Crimson Archer just stared at me, confused. "They're not with me."

"What? But…" I trailed off, staring at the leaking can on the ground.

Crimson Archer put his weapons away. "Look, let's just go talk to PD and see if we can't get this figured out. You got hit in the head pretty hard earlier. We can get you checked out and cleaned up."

I nodded slowly. "Okay."

That might be the safest place to weather whatever came next.

Chapter 13

They had me shackled to a freezing metal table, the gray stone walls stealing away what little light the bare flickering light bulb gave off. PD had let me keep one of my energy drinks, thank god. I took small sips of it, stooping each time just to reach the can, while I waited for Super Human Affairs. They were a smaller department. Most cities had a handful of detectives assigned, typically no more than their hero had rogues. The only exception was Umbra's city. Cion dedicated nearly half of their police force just to deal with all the lunatics their cursed city churned out. Occasionally, even one of their guys turned to the dark side. Well, dark for a cop.

The door clicked open as the head of Spire City's Super Human Affairs walked in. Lieutenant Jason Gray was a formidable man: a six-foot-tall wall of muscle that threatened to rip his shirt open with every minuscule movement, dressed in a black button-up with a red vest. His raven hair was split with a white streak that rumor had it was from a resurrection attempt in his mysterious past. His undeniably fine features were marred from his time in Cion before transferring here. A jagged scar at the corner of his mouth partially exposed his teeth and ran below a blood-red eye patch, ending just above the damaged socket. Gray slapped a file down on the table and took the seat across from me.

"Man, you look like all kinds of shit."

I gestured to the corner of my mouth with my middle finger. Very mature, I know. "What happened here again? Cut yourself shaving?"

Gray cocked an eyebrow as he flipped open the file. "Not your best. Rough night?"

I scowled at him. "Something like that."

"C'mon, Malice. What's the story?"

"It's not in there?"

"I wanna hear it from you."

"You wouldn't believe me if I told you."

Gray rolled his eye. "Christ, man. Be fucking original."

I fidgeted with the handcuffs, not entirely eager to rehash tonight's events. But it wasn't like I had anything better to do while I waited for the next of The False Angel's monsters.

"Fine. Yesterday, or maybe it was the day before. I'm not sure how long it's been. Anyway, Zarael and her Justice Buddies came after me, claiming I killed the transport guys on my last escape. I didn't. I liked them. Well, one of them. But during the ensuing fight, I noticed Zarael was different, wrong."

Gray had taken out a small notepad and was scribbling notes in an ineligible script. "Different how?"

I shrugged, watching my reflection in the mirror do the same. "Her aura was different. Like it was just light, not her power. There was something wrong with her eyes. And she was paler."

Gray nodded and flipped to the next page. "What happened next?"

"I tried to tell the others, but they wouldn't listen. Called me crazy. Probably just chalked it up to a head injury."

Gray paused. "Did you get checked out after the fight?"

I shook my head. "I blacked out after Zarael destroyed my suit. The other heroes just let her do it. When I woke up, she had me chained to the wall in Nove Cerchi."

"The official report says you escaped en route to prison."

I glared at him, sending all my hate into that one silver eye. "Am I really giving off the impression that's what happened to me?"

Gray didn't even flinch, just gestured at me to continue.

"She had me in the solitary wing."

"Oh, the seven sins."

"What?"

"That's what it was called, each arm representing one of the seven deadly sins. The guy that built the prison was a special kind of religious nut." He looked up at me, quickly realizing I wasn't as excited about that as he was. "Go on."

"Once I got out, I met Zarael's guard. The burnt corpses of the two transport guards fused into a monster. I...took care of it."

I had to force myself to continue, though the bloody spot that was once my friend's head haunted me.

"Anyway, I got off the island, and a Coast Guard boat found me. But so did Thalassa. Zarael had changed her, too. She killed the crew, and I killed her."

"Seems fair."

"Then I made it back to shore, got some energy drinks, and The Crimson Douche found me."

Gray studied his notes, occasionally flicking his eye over to the file.

"Well, your story sounds batshit crazy, but you look crazier right now. So, I'll send someone to check out Nove Cerchi and the bay. We'll keep you here for now, just in case."

Relief flooded through my body. I didn't know if I would have survived another attempt to take me to prison. Gray stood to leave as the door flew open and Zarael strutted in, slamming the door closed behind her. The room spun around me and a wave of nausea threatened to make the chicken tenders reappear. But Zarael looked worse than I felt. Her wings had faded from white to an ashy gray, black veins spread into the whites of her eyes. I could just barely detect the faint smell of decay that was lingering in the air.

The False Angel sneered at me. "What's this heathen been telling you?"

Gray studied her, his right arm angling towards his gun. "Oh, we were just shootin' the shit. Talking about…guy stuff." His eye flicked up towards her forehead. "What is that? Some sort of power gem or something?" He pointed at his own head.

I looked up. There was something there. A sickly yellow crystal was embedded in her forehead, just barely peeking out from behind a lock of hair. It was faint, but it looked like there was something burrowing under her skin. How had I missed that?

The False Angel switched her glare to Gray. "Yes, something like that." Her words came out stilted and cold.

Gray looked at me, then back at her. "So, you took Malice here to Nove Cerchi instead of prison? Odd choice."

The fake Zarael scowled, her yellow eyes staring daggers at me. She wrapped a hand around the hilt of her sword. "Is that what he told you?"

Gray gave a quick nod.

"And you believe him?"

He shrugged.

"Whatever I did, trust that it was necessary."

Gray sighed and shook his head. "Any other day of the week, I just might."

Without so much as a second thought, he pulled out his gun and aimed it directly at The False Angel.

"But you don't look right, Zee."

A shot rang out, and everything seemed to happen in slow motion. Shards of yellow filled the air, crackling with a sinister energy as The False Angel dropped to her knees and a familiar glow filled the room. I leapt from my chair and caught her right as she threatened to collapse. I cupped her face in my hand. When her eyes opened and her golden irises met mine, the world seemed to blur.

"Is it…"

Zarael, the real Zarael, smiled and nodded. "It's me."

Something in my chest tore. Her arms wrapped around me as I hugged her close.

"I'll change now, I promise. For you. I'll be a better man, build a better world. Just for you." I moved back and met her gaze again. "I will be perfect for you."

Chapter 14

For her, I faced restitution for my actions.

The first month, they officially interred me back in Nove Cerchi with Zarael acting as warden. By the second month, I had made enough living metal to transform my penitentiary into something new. Zarael and I watched together as the obsidian liquid released itself upon the decrepit prison. It crawled over the watchtower and flowed into the seven sins, transforming Nove Cerchi into my citadel. Now the actual work could begin.

I had free rein to do what I wanted, as long as I kept good on my promises to Zarael. Over the course of the next year, Spire City became my utopia. Living metal construction took over crumbling buildings and restored them beyond what they once were. Decrepit lots became homes for those who needed them. I spent my days toiling in my workshop, fabricating revolutionary inventions. Changing the world. But my nights belonged to her. It started small. There was obviously some tension after her brief possession. She wouldn't linger after checking in on me, wouldn't make eye contact. She limited her responses to one-word answers. But gradually, the wall cracked and broke.

She would stand silently watching whenever I'd get lost in

my work. On particularly long nights, there would be food or water left for me to find, a reminder to take a break. Her stays became longer. We talked for hours, voices echoing off the walls, discussing everything and nothing. She would even talk to me while I worked, genuinely curious about what I was doing. An accidental brush against a hand sent a spark between us, blood rushing to our cheeks like blushing teenagers. Inadvertent touches turned into stolen glances, and stolen glances turned into unmistakable longing.

Zarael was "monitoring" me tonight, perched atop one of my workshop counters, one leg pulled up to rest her arm on. I was lost in my work, hands stained with ink, papers covered in my illegible scribbling piled on my desk. While she was doing her best to stay quiet, I could still feel her watching me like a stray thought pushed to the back of my mind. It didn't help that she kept bouncing her heel against the wall, either.

"You're restless," I said, not looking away from my work.

"I'm bored."

I shrugged. "Same thing."

"Maybe, but you just had to use the bigger word for it."

A dull thud came from behind me as Zarael launched herself off the counter. A second later, my chair spun around, putting me face to face with the Guardian Angel of Spire City. Golden flame enveloped her, burning away her armor and wings. She was left in her "street clothes," a white tee with jeans and a leather jacket.

"Let's do something."

I grabbed a golden ember off her shoulder as it faded away into nothingness. "If you would just let me study your armor, I could make something fantastic."

Zarael rolled her eyes at me. "No shop talk. Fun talk. Now."

"Technically, I'm not supposed to leave the island."

"Then we'll do something on the stupid island!" she yelled back at me, already out of the workshop.

We found ourselves wandering the beach, fingers tentatively reaching for the others. There were no costumes or masks here. No Malice and Zarael. Just me and Zee. The night sky was an endless abyss, speckled with bright stars twinkling against the inky blackness. As we both looked up in awe at the sea of stars above us, I found my gaze wandering back to her. She was perfect. Even as the wind tousled her hair, it seemed to frame her face in an ivory halo. Her eyes slowly shifted to meet mine, her golden irises briefly flicking downward before staring back at me. In that moment, time slid to a standstill. One arm snaked around her waist, pulling her into me. Even without her aura visible, she radiated warmth and comfort. I brushed away nothing in particular and cupped her face. I could feel the heat of her breath on mine, and the scent of oranges filled the air between us. Our lips brushed against each other, cautious and uncertain. We laughed off the uncomfortable moment, the sound carrying through the night. But that quick touch sparked a fire. Our lips moved in tandem, clinging together, refusing to break apart. I could feel her muscles tense, and a shiver ran down her spine. I knew she felt what I did. Hunger. Craving. In that moment, all I wanted was her. All I needed was her.

I pressed my body into hers as we drifted to the ground, both of us clawing at our suddenly constricting clothing. My mouth ran down her neck, sucking on the tender flesh, as my hands caressed her bare skin. I went lower and lower, propping her legs up on my shoulders. I had to taste her. Her fingers ran through my hair, wrapping around the dark curls. She was grinding her hips into me as I ran my tongue over her, spelling any word that came to mind. My chin was slick as she hooked a finger under it, fixing me in her golden-eyed stare. Her irises glowed in the dark, begging me to come to her. I crawled to her, letting her legs slide under my arms and wrap around my waist. She licked at my face, running her tongue along my chin, tasting herself before pressing her lips back to mine. Her hand slipped down my chest as she slid her tongue into my mouth. She wrapped her fingers around me and guided me inside her. The world pulsed bright around us. All my senses faded into her.

***

I held her in my arms, running a hand over the well-defined muscle. When you swing a sword all day, you're bound to bulk up. She had summoned her aura, wrapping the two of us in a golden cocoon shuttered away from the rest of the world. I held my breath, just wanting to feel her chest rise and fall as she lay next to me.

"What are you doing, weirdo?"

I exhaled just before my lungs started burning. "Just listening to you breathe."

"Hmm." She burrowed herself tighter in my arms.

"What about you? What are you doing?"

She smiled, keeping her eyes closed like she was enjoying a particularly good dream. "Just thinking."

"Thinking about what?"

Her eyes flickered open as she stared up at me. "I think I love you, John."

No one had told me before, not romantically, at least. There was a strange feeling in my chest. Something new. "I think I

61

love you too, Zee. I think, if I ever lost you, I would raze this world to the ground. I don't want to live in a world without you in it."

She cuddled closer to me. "That almost sounds like something a villain would say."

"Almost."

We just lay there in silence, letting our words sink in. I chuckled as realization dawned on me.

"What?"

I looked down at her. "We just said 'I love you,' but we don't know each other's names."

She laughed, but it was off. Almost uncertain.

"So, what is it?"

"Hmm?"

"Your name. Your real name."

Her body tensed as the world suddenly went cold. "Why does it matter?"

I chuckled again, uneasy now. Had I made her mad? "I was just curious. It's been over a year since that crystal possessed you, and we're still calling each other John and Zee like that first night."

"John's the name in your file."

"But it's not my name. John Doe is merely a placeholder, a name for the unknown."

"So who are you?"

"I—" I wanted to tell her, I did. But something was off. "I—"

"God, you're so boring! And unbearably dense. Do you have to question every fucking thing?"

"Wha—"

Zarael drove her hand into my chest, splitting apart flesh and bone. She pulled back hard, taking my heart with her. My heart was still beating in her hand as she stood up, blood dripping down to her elbow. Her eyes changed, reverting to that sickly yellow, the whites fading to black.

"I gave you the girl, gave you a whole little island to play in, and you can't just leave it be?"

The world distorted. The sky started changing colors at random. Tiny hands of earth formed and dragged me down into the ground. My head and arms poked out of the sand, grit painfully rubbing into my gaping chest wound.

"Wha—"

"Wha, wha, wha! Your head is so far up your own ass, I don't know how you breathe!" An evil grin spread across her face. "So let's change that."

The False Angel snapped her fingers, and I was sinking farther into the earth, the grainy soil forcing itself into my mouth. The earth clawed at me, tearing the flesh, snapping my bones like dried twigs. She just watched with sick glee, snacking on my heart.

Chapter 15

I couldn't breathe. I was clawing at my throat, desperate to get air in any way I could. My nails scraped against the flesh, leaving red streaks in their wake. My body thrashed from side to side, desperate to escape whatever new prison I was in. Something gave way beneath me, and my stomach dropped as I fell into nothingness. My hands jerked upright, bound to something above me. With a desperate gasp, I filled my lungs with stale, freezing air. My eyes flew open. I was back in the interrogation room.

All my writhing had knocked the chair over, leaving me on the concrete floor. My hands were still chained to the table, keeping my upper body mostly off the floor. I scrambled up as best I could, mostly leaning on the table. My legs were strangely numb, and my head felt like it was in a haze. My little fit had provided The False Angel with an opportunity, causing Gray to take his eye off of her. I managed to get to my feet, hunched over with my hands still bound, just as Zarael's blade sliced through Gray's arm, severing it just above the elbow. Blood arced across the table, some of it spraying my face. Gray's arm flopped onto the floor, the gun still clenched in his hand. He just stood there, frozen, more sanguine fluid lazily dripping from the stump. A scream tried to escape his lips, but something closer to a whimper came out. Gray's one eye rolled into the back of his head as he collapsed onto the floor.

The False Angel's face distorted with rage, every ounce of it aimed at me, her true face writhing underneath the appropriated flesh. Her wings spread open, filling the room and barring anything from going in or out. She seemed larger now, an imposing presence that permeated the room. This close, I could see that the corruption from her possession had spread further through her body since entering the room. A handful of feathers had turned completely black, speckling throughout the graying wings. Those last moments in her dream world had turned the whites of her eyes completely black, but the darkness had spread into her face as thin veins.

Zarael slowly advanced, flames flickering weakly along her sword. She ran the blade through the table, sending scalding drops of liquefied metal cascading onto the floor. The flames disappeared just before reaching the bar that pinned my handcuffs to the table. As she withdrew her blade, the table buckled, dragging me to my knees and bending the bar into a V with the center link of my handcuffs held by its point. The False Angel aimed the tip of her sword right at my Adam's apple, the heat emanating off the blade forcing me to crane my head up and stare into those demonic eyes.

That cruel smirk played across her lips. "You just couldn't leave well enough alone. You broke all my toys. Seems only fair I get to break you."

The interrogation room window exploded, sending shards of one-way glass into Zarael's back. A flurry of throwing knives followed, each one piercing The False Angel's wings. The knives opened up pulsing wounds ringed in black, healing just as fast as they formed. Black ichor dripped from the fake Zarael's back as the glass shards were pushed out onto the floor.

"Looks like you get a stay of execution. I have a new toy to play with." Zarael turned to face her attacker, folding her wings back behind her. "I was hoping you'd make another appearance."

Umbra crouched in the empty frame. Their costume was shredded, revealing pale skin and hastily bandaged wounds. Even the mesh that covered their head was torn, revealing the lower half of their face. They bared their teeth and readied three more knives in each hand, brandishing them like claws. With a roar, they leapt at The False Angel, fists aimed at her chest. Zarael let out a sigh. Her hand shot up faster than any normal human's could, maybe even faster than the real Zarael could, and caught Umbra by their exposed mouth.

The False Angel shook her head, scolding the trapped hero. "Now, there's no need for that. I'm just going to make you fit to play with." Her hand melted into their face, fusing to the flesh, armor and all. Umbra's body went slack, their limbs just dangling in the air.

Zarael frowned, disappointed with whatever she found inside Umbra. "Nothing really special about you, is there? I can fix that."

Umbra's body seized as their limbs stretched and thinned. Their neck almost seemed to drip as it extended, followed by their torso. Zarael gathered dim golden light in her other hand and ran it over Umbra's ruined uniform. Armor and fabric melted and reformed, forming a shiny black carapace. Their hyperextended fingers turned into needle-like claws. The mesh around their head receded, forming a helmet that left their eyes and mouth exposed.

The False Angel released them, letting their body crumple to the ground like a rag doll as she flicked the melted flesh off her fingers with a look of disgust. Two lidless eyes stared blankly into space, now identical to the fake Zarael's. Umbra's chest heaved, their eyes spinning wildly and out of sync, like a coked-out chameleon. They sat up, limbs pointing in all different directions. Umbra stood shakily on their thin legs, arms swaying slightly at their sides. The transformation had left their mouth sealed behind a mass of twisted flesh. They flexed their jaw once, twice, the sealed dermis refusing to open. Umbra dug their new claws into what had once been their mouth, blood pouring down their chin. They found purchase and pulled down on their jaw, revealing large rounded teeth that their ragged lips had no hope of covering. They didn't scream. All they could do was make a wet, wheezing sound. Like the air couldn't escape their lungs fast enough.

"Huuuuuuuh…huuuuuh…huuuuuh."

Crimson Archer decided now was the best time to make his reappearance, marching into the room with two pizza boxes in his hands and a dumbass smile on his face. His smile dropped as his single brain cell fully took in what was going on. Zarael nodded at the door.

"Go play."

Umbra bolted past the mystified archer, knocking the pizzas out of his hands and splattering them across the floor. Crimson Archer just stood and whimpered as The False Angel brushed past him, not even bothering to acknowledge him. She shot a look at me as the world beyond this room went dark, masking her exit.

Then the screaming started.

Chapter 16

"Dude, what the fuck is going on?"

World's finest indeed.

"I was right. You were wrong. Nothing new. Get me out of these?"

Crimson Archer whipped his head back and forth, looking at me, then at the darkened precinct. If he sped up, he could probably get airborne. He winced as another scream rang out, not realizing that his delay wasn't helping anyone. Something finally clicked in that empty skull.

"Yeah, okay. Let me get my lock-picking arrow."

Of course. "Your what?"

"Lock-picking arrow?"

Why was he looking at me like that's a normal thing to say? "You don't have a lock-picking set? Or better yet, just a handcuff key?"

He shook his head and started digging through his quiver.

"Just get Gray's keys. He's not going to need them anymore."

He nodded and cautiously made his way over to the wounded officer, his steps slow and deliberate. Archer reached for the keys on Gray's belt, pausing just before he took them. He pressed a hand to Gray's neck.

"Hey, he's still alive."

I rolled my eyes. "So fix him up real quick, then get. Me. Out. Of. These."

"Okay, I have an arrow for this."

"You're a superhero and you don't know any first aid? Not even something basic for crisis situations?"

"I have the arrows do it for me!"

I'll kill him. No one could ever trace it back to me. Oh no, the last time I saw him, the Umbra monster was eating him. Pretty sure Zarael barbecued him just for fun. No one would ever know. I let out a tired, heavy sigh that echoed in the air. Pretty sure I felt a blood vessel burst. I just needed him to get me out of the handcuffs. And I suppose it wouldn't hurt my case if Gray was alive. Come to think of it, he could probably track Zarael. I needed to keep calm if any of that was going to happen. He looked like he'd break down crying if I yelled at him.

"Fine. Just hurry."

He nodded, pulled an arrow from his quiver, and began fidgeting with some buttons on the side. "I'm going to cauterize the wound."

"Wait, I think you skipped a few steps—"

Gray let out a bloodcurdling scream as Crimson Archer jammed the tip of his arrow into the stump, setting off something that looked weirdly like a road flare. Thankfully, he didn't use his bow to shoot Gray. I tried to cover my face as the smell of burnt flesh filled the room and chicken-flavored vomit threatened to spew from my mouth. My ribs ached, the sickly sweet scent bringing back the memories of my fight with Curtis. It felt like weeks had passed since this whole thing started, even though it had only been a few hours. Archer pressed another button on the arrow, spraying some sort of foam into the burnt flesh. Gray let out a hiss of pain, then passed back out, crumpling into a pile next to a pool of his own blood. I leaned forward as best as I could, straining to listen for any sound or catch any movement to show he was breathing.

"Is he dead?"

Gray made a low, guttural sound and rolled over, almost like a response to my question. Small favors, I suppose. "Alright. Now uncuff me and we can go deal with this."

Crimson Archer stood up, slowly turning to face me. "About that."

He knocked an arrow and fired, cutting through the bar that pinned me. I felt the air move as the arrow flew past me, bouncing off the wall and clattering onto the stone floor.

"I think I like you better in cuffs."

The shock had worn off, pushing him from paralyzing numbness to survival mode. He had one known and one unknown enemy flanking him. He was going to keep what he could control locked down for as long as he could. Maybe there were a few extra brain cells in there, but now was definitely not the time to use them. I had to be extremely careful if I wanted him on my side. Not everyone wields power in a crisis well.

I slid the chain of my handcuffs out through the broken bar, keeping my hands open and in view. "Okay, okay."

I stood up slowly, relief flowing down my back and into my legs. I pushed a little more than I needed to, popping my knees and spine. Crimson Archer flinched with each pop. He was on edge. The False Angel's attack may have finally turned him into something dangerous. Archer's face contorted with fear as he quickly dropped his bow from his shoulder, nocking an arrow as he sprinted towards the door. A chill ran down my spine as I realized what he'd heard. Nothing. The screams had stopped, leaving an unnatural silence hanging in the air.

Archer stifled a cry of rage. "Come on! We spent too long fucking around in here. We have to go find anyone who made it out."

"So far, these things haven't left any survivors."

Crimson Archer glared back at me. "Well, you're still here, aren't you? Up front, Malice."

Reluctantly, I stepped out into the darkness of the precinct. My contacts reacted to the shadows, gradually turning the world from black to bright green. As I ventured down the hall, I could hear my own footsteps echoing in the emptiness.

"Alright," I called back. "Looks clear."

When I looked back to see if Archer was behind me, the world turned white. A scorching pain shot through my skull, like my optic nerves themselves were on fire. I doubled over in pain, clapping my hands over my eyes so my contacts could readjust.

"What is that?"

"Flashlight arrow. How else am I supposed to see?"

"That stupid domino mask doesn't have night vision?"

"No."

I could hear the contempt in his voice. This new attitude was going to be a problem.

"Turn it off. That's a beacon that leads straight to us."

He scoffed at me. "And trust you to guide me? I don't think so. Now move!" He shoved me, the force slamming me into the wall. My other injuries joined in the pain, singing together like a sadistic symphony. I grit my teeth and marched on, not wanting to shoot a look back at the Archer and blind myself again because of his arrogance.

The hallway gave way to a small staircase that led up to the bullpen. The steps were wet and slick. Even with the night vision coloring the world in different shades of green, it wasn't hard to tell what we were walking through. As we approached the door to the bullpen, I had to shield my eyes from the intense glare of Crimson Archer's light reflecting off the metal.

I tried the door, slowly turning the handle. It made a soft click as it opened but stopped a few inches in. I swung the door back, then opened it again, adding just a little more force. Something hanging off the other side of the door leaned forward, then fell back with a quiet thud. As I went to repeat the process, Crimson Archer shoved me to the side and slammed his foot into the door, sending it flying open with an explosive crash. I flinched as he glared at me, turning away as he swung the light in my direction.

"There's no time for this pussy shit."

I turned back to see Umbra's monumental carnage. They had unintentionally blocked the door with one of many mutilated corpses. The body was slumped on the floor now, thrown forward by Crimson Archer's assault on the door. Weeping lacerations peered out through the ripped uniform, adding to the sanguine fluid on the floor. A severed arm swung in and out of view, clutching the doorknob in death. Crimson Archer was ahead of me, swinging his light over the slaughter. Ruined corpses littered the ground, all blending together in my dull green vision. There weren't a lot of officers on the night shift, but Umbra managed to turn each and every one of them into a mountain of broken bones and exposed intestines. Desks and cubicle walls formed a crooked perimeter for Umbra's horde. Blood and guts hung off of just about every surface possible. Gore caked the floor, turning it into a paradoxical combination that clung to your shoes and made the tile slick. The most worrying part of this entire scene, however, was that Umbra was nowhere to be found.

Crimson Archer kicked one of the upturned desks. "Where the fuck are they?"

I could feel my own rage boiling back to the surface, melting through the restraint I'd been showing Archer so far. "This is not the time for a tantrum!" I hissed at him, barely keeping my voice at a whisper. "Consider us lucky they're not here. I've killed two of these things so far, barely escaping with my life each time."

Crimson Archer rushed me, intentionally shining his light into my eyes. "You think you's so fucking smart, huh?" He dropped the light and let my eyes recover before bringing it back up. "Malice knows better than everyone, huh?"

I should have stopped him, or at least turned off my night vision, but I swear I saw—

Another flash of light blinded me again. I blocked him out, focusing on the wall behind him. Sure enough, something moved.

Another flash. Spots swam in my vision. Maybe that's all it was, just aftereffects of the Archer's light.

Another flash. No, there they were, clinging to the wall like an insect. Umbra watched as Crimson Archer yelled at me, staring with dead eyes.

Another flash. They were crawling down the wall now, slow and deliberate. Their spindly limbs carried them across the blood-splattered surface, the sharp joints angled above their body.

Another flash. My vision was gradually shrinking to one small point. I couldn't see anything around or beyond Crimson Archer's red and sweating face, spittle flying with each obscenity. Umbra's armored claws floated into view, their sharp fingers just barely hovering an inch away from Crimson Archer's head.

Archer brought his light for another flash, his eye flicking to the side as he brought his arm up. My vision turned white as Umbra clamped their claws around Crimson Archer's head. A crack echoed throughout the room, followed by a dull thump. I stumbled back blindly, slipping on guts and gore. The air was forced from my lungs as I slammed into the floor, sliding a few inches back through the blood. I scrambled back, desperate to escape whatever attack was coming.

My vision swam back into focus. Umbra crouched next to Crimson Archer's body, tugging on one of his arms. The former hero grew frustrated as the arm dislocated, but the flesh refused to tear. Umbra clamped their jaws around the Archer's shoulder, gnawing through the muscle and bone. Blood dripped down their face as the arm separated from the rest of the body with a wet squelching noise. Umbra bit down and tore a hunk of flesh off, chewing it with their mouth wide open as they stared at me. I crept to my feet, not even daring to blink in fear of losing sight of Umbra. My eyes burned, but Umbra just sat there, devouring their former teammate. I let my gaze drift down, eyeing my best chance at getting something to defend myself with. Crimson Archer's bow was right in front of me, ready to be taken. His quiver was a different and much more challenging story. I inched forward, gingerly wrapping my hand around the bow. Umbra didn't even flinch. They didn't seem to care, were too engrossed in their "food." I slid the bow over my shoulder and pushed forward, slowly closing the distance between myself and Umbra.

In just a few moments, I was right there, staring into Umbra's eyes. A blast of heat hit me in the face with each nauseating bite.

I slid my fingers under the quiver's strap. I stopped as my hand brushed against Crimson Archer's chest, feeling a slight rise and fall. My gaze drifted from Umbra down to the Archer. He stared back at me, pleading with his eyes. Umbra had merely paralyzed him, leaving him alive as they feasted on him.

I pressed my thumb into the quick release button on the quiver's strap, daring to jerk it away from the still breathing Archer. Umbra still stared, completely focused on Crimson Archer's arm. I brought the quiver clasps over my chest, connecting the two pieces and securing it to my back. An idiotic flash of heroism surged through me, and I leapt for Crimson Archer's other arm. As my hand grabbed his, Umbra broke from their meal. Umbra swung the severed arm at me, chasing me back with a spray of blood. I stumbled back, caught myself, and sprinted past Umbra and their captive. Crimson Archer was a lost cause. An ear-splitting screech followed me as I ran farther into the darkened precinct.

Chapter 17

I bolted down the first hallway I saw, searching a for a stairwell. I didn't know the precinct's layout well, but heading down should get me to an exit or the garage, if I was lucky. Given how the rest of the night had gone, I wasn't holding my breath.

The shadows were in constant motion, writhing and twisting around. Some even looked like they were trying to take shape, blindly grasping after me. Pain shot down my left arm, almost causing me to lose Crimson Archer's bow. I tightened my grip and chanced a glance back. Thin marks lined my shoulder, red and angry. Not parallel to each other, like a swipe from Umbra would be. These were wild, berserk. A shiver ran down my spine. I could feel something behind me, just out of sight. This hallway wasn't right. I needed out of here ASAP.

As quickly as I thought it, the door to the stairwell came into view. Strange, but I didn't think I had time to give this gift horse's mouth a thorough study. I wrenched the door open, and the shadows surged forward. Spears of living darkness flew at me, perforating the door as I slammed it shut behind me. The shadow blades oozed through the points of entry, pooling together as they reached the stone floor. I bolted down the stairs, skipping every other step.

A quick glance over the side revealed four flights to the garage.

Not terrible. I chanced a look back, and there stood Umbra. They stood statuesque at the top of the stair, claws twitching at their sides. A mass of shadows hung above them, pulsing and beating like a massive heart. Dark liquid dripped from the shadow heart, the black spots it left spreading and branching into veins. I gripped the railing, knuckles white as I stood frozen. I didn't even remember stopping. A black drop landed on my hand, and pain shocked me back into motion. Its acidic touch burned through my skin, leaving a trail of pink marks where its branches had dug in.

As I reached the third landing, Umbra twitched and began their descent. If they wanted to, they could be on me in seconds. Launching myself over the railing, I hit the ground in a crouch, the black liquid splattering against me in the few seconds I stopped. I slammed into the double doors, barreling into the stagnant heat of the garage. I had my pick of identical cruisers. Now I just had to get one started.

A muffled crack reverberated from behind me. The double doors exploded out, flying off their hinges. I was tired, my body ached and burned. But running wouldn't help me now. I dredged up every scrap of anger I had, letting it fuel me once again. Slowly, I turned to face my pursuer, nocking an arrow as I did. Umbra stood in the doorway, made visible by my pale green vision. The shadow heart bled over them, adding armor to their rail-thin frame. Thick plate formed around their shoulders and flowed over their chest. The helm they wore was an intricate design of sharp angles, completely concealing their face, with thin lenses that shaded their eyes. Umbra took a single step forward, and the world turned a bright, painful white. I dropped to my knees, my head threatening to crack open. My weapon fell to the floor with a loud clatter as I clapped my hands over my eyes. As the pain subsided, I opened my eyes to absolute darkness.

Gradually, my contacts adjusted to this new light. Even with their help, spots were floating in my blurred vision. Some of the garage's overhead lights had come back on, carving out a small patch among the raging storm of shadows that now encircled me. The dark was constantly in motion, forming faces screaming in silence or hands clawing at me. No light moved in or out.

Carefully, I reached for the bow, slowly wrapping my fingers around it. Once I had it in hand, I went back for the discarded arrow. The shadows stilled, full stop. I barely had time to take a breath before the darkness lunged at me, a sea of the damned screaming within it. I kept my eyes and mouth covered, not wanting anything to reach inside. The shadows rocked me side to side, launched me up and down. They were trying to keep me disoriented.

After a few minutes in the torrent, the shadows slammed me into something solid and let me drop. I opened one eye, then the other, my eyelids flickering like something was going to fly into them. I was in another circle of light, the shadows pulsing around me. Umbra had studied my interaction with Crimson Archer, hoped to turn my night vision into their own torture device. Umbra fought against the most twisted and brutal of this world's villains, had to get into their heads constantly. With that knowledge and their new powers, stripped of their convictions, The False Angel had created a whole other league of monster.

There was no time to think, just react. The shadows stilled, and I fired off an arrow just as the darkness came at me. A boxing glove arrow struck one of the police cruisers, setting off its alarm. Lights flashed as the alarmed screeched into the garage. Umbra howled in response, quickly disabling the lights. Only the lights. The shadows stilled again, preparing to move. I strung an arrow and…nothing. I relaxed just a bit, only for the shadows to come crashing down on me from above. That was the game. Keep me alert and jumping at the slightest movement. The shadows slammed me into the ceiling, letting me fall to the floor. I jumped to my feet, holding my breath in anticipation of the next attack. I prayed this would be a longer one as I pulled two more arrows from the quiver. My heart pounded in my chest as I searched for any sign of what the arrows actually did. Out of the three, two looked like they'd work for what I had in mind. I fired both off in the direction where I thought the car alarm's blare was coming from, and where Umbra still may be.

The first began giving off a steady beeping sound, probably meant to draw in unsuspecting enemies. The second flashed SOS in morse code, scarlet light cutting through the darkness. Umbra stayed silent this time, but I could just about make them out as they moved towards the arrows. With a deafening crunch, the second arrow stopped giving off its silent message. Umbra left the other arrow untouched. For the first time in this hellish night, I let a smile break across my face.

"I can work with that."

Umbra didn't give me the chance to. The shadows surged from behind me, pulling me towards their master. I tried to plant my feet and struggle against them, but the dark legion was many, and I was one. Umbra's hand burst from the shadows, their thin fingers wrapping around my head. They took Crimson Archer's bow from me, and the garage echoed with the sound of splintering wood. No matter. That was just one tool. Umbra tossed me back into the shadow, letting the torrent shake me furiously through the artificial night. They let the shadows play with me longer this time. I felt the sharp pain of claws raking across my back, and teeth sinking into my flesh. After being trapped in the darkness for what felt like an eternity, Umbra unceremoniously dumped me back onto the cold, hard stone floor.

I grit my teeth and crawled onto my hands and knees, refusing to give Umbra the satisfaction of seeing me defeated. They hadn't beaten me. I still had plenty of arrows. I just needed to be closer to use them now. The lights above started flickering, no longer content with one still beam.

I stretched, trying to push myself and prepare for the next assault. And there, in the darkness, my fingers wrapped around a discarded arrow. I brought it up to my face and carefully studied it to determine its purpose. There were no markings on it, just a soda-can-sized canister built just below the arrowhead. It would have to do. The light above me finally gave out, stranding me in the dark. I waited for the attack, trying my best to seem helpless and inviting. The tense anticipation of an attack subsided as the minutes ticked by, and still, nothing happened. Frustrated, I clambered to my feet, spinning around in a desperate search for Umbra. My night vision gradually came back, turning the thick shadows that surrounded me green. Still, nothing. The moment I took a step forward, Umbra pounced on me. One thin claw gripped my shirt in a ball, yanking me down before pulling me back up. Umbra held me in front of them, studying me with their wild eyes. Their mouth fell open, their jaws and lips rung in armor. Saliva ran down their squared teeth, eager to tear into my flesh.

I didn't give them the chance. The sound of flesh tearing echoed as I jammed the arrow into their mouth, pinning their tongue to the bottom of their jaw. An angry roar rumbled in their chest just as the air erupted with heat and pure white light. Umbra dropped me, screeching in agony as the white phosphorus burned in their mouth and down into their throat. The shadows all around us writhed as if in pain, mirroring their master. Umbra's shadow armor melted from their lean body, evaporating into nothingness. Umbra clawed at their throat, trying to dislodge the arrow. The sickly sweet scent of burnt flesh filled the air as they finally stopped screaming. I stared down at them, realization dawning on me.

"I think I just committed a war crime."

Chapter 18

Three of the world's greatest heroes were dead, two of them by my hand. One more wouldn't change my place in Hell.

Stealing a police cruiser was easy. I'm sure Crimson Archer had some kind of carjacking arrow in his bag of deus ex machina. But I refused to justify the creation of his more ridiculous arrows, even in death. No more than I already had, at least. Besides, it wasn't like the keys were hard to find. Unclaimed sets hung on a pegboard just off of the bullpen. I chose the set with the least amount of blood and gore on them. Finding the cruiser itself was a whole other story. The fob was useless unless I aimed it directly at the car. Kinda defeated the point. It was clearly an older vehicle; dents pockmarked the body with rust peeking out from chipped paint. But it was the same gas guzzling muscle car every station just had to have. I slid into the driver's seat, tossing in Crimson Archer's quiver beside me. Not that I was ever going to use it again; it was just a backup.

It took a few tries to get the car started. As I turned the key, I could feel it catch and stick, like it was struggling to ignite the engine. I contemplated grabbing another set, but I'd wasted too much time already. The key nearly broke off in the ignition before the car finally came to life with a roar that filled the garage.

The engine growled as I pulled out onto the street. I cruised slowly in the dark. I could've used the siren and the flashing lights to get to my destination faster, but I didn't want to draw attention to myself. Anyone who had avoided the massacre might not be too happy to find the city's most notorious villain in a stolen police cruiser. That and a precinct full of bodies would be all the excuse they needed to dole out their own justice. And...I had no idea how I was going to face The False Angel.

She'd been toying with me for the entire night, and I knew next to nothing about her. As far as powers went, she seemed to have an approximation of Zarael's. It could be she couldn't access the full power of the golden plate. Not only could she manipulate organic matter, the fake Zarael also had immense psychic abilities. Trapping me in a dream world and controlling a dead puppet were one thing, but completely taking over a living being was the true testament of her power. Thalassa had been a gentle being. She visited schools, helped clean up her villains' messes. She believed all life was sacred. Even Umbra was a symbol of hope and change in their city, reserving any brutality they had for the most far gone of their rogues. And The False Angel could twist their minds without breaking a sweat. She could also heal, at least from minor wounds.

The tires bumped against the curb, pulling me from my thoughts. Headlights illuminated the worn obsidian doors of my cathedral. I slung the quiver over one shoulder as I exited the car, scanning my surroundings for any more of The False Angel's puppets. I dragged myself up the steps and forced the doors open. They felt heavier than before. Something broke inside me as I looked over my home.

The rain started up again as if on cue. Moonlight illuminated the shards of broken glass, making a glittering pathway to the ruins of my workstation. The tables that held everything had been upended and tossed to the side. Tools were scattered across the floor. Monitors were cut in half. The computer towers had been broken down into their individual pieces, their hard drives stolen. At the center of it all was the glass tube that had once held my living metal. The glass itself had been shattered, leaving a few broken shards jutting up from the base. Blade marks carved through the metal, exposing the inner workings.

I forced myself forward, glass crunching beneath my feet. I dropped to my knees, running a hand over the base. The last of the living metal was supposed to be hidden within the base, but it was damaged and powerless, effectively sealing it away. All I needed was a little space, and what remained of my armor would be free. I slammed a fist into the center. Then the other. Again and again. My knuckles split open, and blood painted the metal. Something clicked in my head, and I cursed my stupidity. I tore the quiver off my back and dumped its contents onto the floor. A basic steel tipped arrow glinted in the moonlight. A mad grin spread across my face as I took the arrow in both hands, aiming for the bloody bullseye. I brought it down hard, the tip finding a seam in the metal it could burrow into. The metal shaft bent as I pushed it farther with every ounce of strength I had left. The black liquid metal spurted out like blood in a wound, climbing up the arrow and wrapping around my arms.

The living metal that made up my cape wasn't very much. Thin armor formed over the backs of my hands, then up my forearms, securing themselves with chains. Four short blades protruded by my knuckles, providing me with some basic offense. That was all I could afford if I still wanted some basic weapons, too. I flexed my fingers, studying my sparse defenses.

I let out a weary sigh. "It'll have to do."

A cold mirthless laugh echoed through the ransacked cathedral, causing every hair on my body to stand on end.

"So, there was some of your black goo left."

I spun around, the living metal writhing, to face The False Angel. She perched in the stone circle where the stained glass had been, black wings wrapped around her. Those sickly yellow eyes glowed in onyx pupils.

"Now, what are you going to do?"

I glared at her, that white-hot fury forming in my chest again, burning away all fatigue. "Why?"

She laughed again and dropped to the floor, moving more like a shadow than a flesh-and-blood being. "Why what?"

"Why are you doing this to me?" I yelled, letting my anger lace my words.

A thin smile crawled across her face. "Oh, I don't know. Maybe this is just the real Zarael. Maybe I was just bored. Or maybe you're just such a bad person that this is all some cosmic punishment for your actions. Or maybe, just maybe, this isn't all about you. Not everything happens for a reason."

I struck out at her twice. The sword I hadn't even seen her draw deflected each time, sparks flying off my knuckle blades. She cocked her head to the side and looked at me like I was a sad puppy.

"Oh, look at you. You're just a child, lashing out because life isn't fair."

She reached out and caressed my face. "It doesn't have to be this way. We could have whatever you and Zarael had."

She tried to contort her face into something that cared. But there was no compassion in her eyes, no warmth to her touch.

"There wasn't anything between us. You made sure of that."

I struck out again, finally connecting. Four thin slashes marred the graying flesh of her neck. There was no blood, nothing dripped from the cuts, just darkness. The False Angel sighed as the skin knitted itself back together and drove her sword into the ground, backing away.

"This form is so limiting. I don't know how you humans get things done. But I think there's room for improvement."

Blood welled at her fingertips as the nails fell off, replaced by thin obsidian claws. She cut into her own flesh, one vertical line on her forehead and two angled at each corner of her mouth. The slits opened up to reveal three fresh eyes, black ichor dripping from their newly formed sockets. I dropped to one knee as my ears popped violently, an unholy pressure filling the room. Her wings spasmed and twisted until they broke apart, lengthening with each tear. When they were done, six sets of long black wings crowded her back and stretched across the room. The skin on her forehead broke open as a wicked-looking crown of antlers grew out. Her knees buckled forward as her legs snapped in half, each segment growing longer and ripping flesh. Three-toed talons burst through her boots. Muscle bulged underneath her armor, threatening to tear through the fabric. My eyes watered. It hurt just to look at her.

"What are you?"

She smiled, I think. Her "face" was slipping off of her skull. "An angel to some, demon to others. I've even been revered as a god once or twice. But for you… well, it won't really matter."

Her voice had been reduced to a horrible grinding sound. Deep and high, gravelly. Like a chainsaw cutting through stone.

She swung an arm out, her skin and uniform ripping as it stretched to reach me. Violet writhing muscle appeared in the tear. I tried to dodge out of the way, but her claw hit home and dug into my thigh. A scream of pain escaped from my lips as she dragged me across the floor, the alien muscle pulsing as it reeled back into its host. The False Angel flapped her wings as I drew close, pulling me upside down into the air. Her limp arm flung me across the room with surprising force, sending me tumbling head over heels through empty space. I landed in the discarded pews, the air forced from my lungs. Blood dripped from the wound on my leg. I rolled over on my side, desperately trying to get a breath of air. The fake Zarael hung in the air, waiting for my next move.

Chapter 19

The living metal writhed, practically begging me to use it. It was the reason I came back here, after all. I pushed myself to my feet, doing my best not to put too much weight on my injured leg. There wasn't enough to make anything big with it, but maybe…

I sacrificed my left gauntlet, melding it into a sickle and attaching it to the chain on my right arm. The False Angel watched as I limped back towards her, the blade hanging at my side. Dark energy crackled along the curve of the sickle.

"Alright," I said, my voice barely a rasp. "Come on then."

The fake Zarael flew at me as I spun my weapon in a circle and launched it at her, the energy thrumming audibly now. She arced away gracefully, soaring back up towards the roof. But the sickle connected. She spasmed in the air, trying to get away from me as the energy pulsed into her body. The living metal continued to extend itself, forming more and more links until it was completely taut. I wrapped around both hands and pulled, bringing The Angel back down to earth. She spun around and—

And smiled. "Kidding."

She held the sickle in her right hand, the purple muscle of her true self winding itself into each link of the chain. The sickle burst into a sickly yellow flame, racing down the chain towards me. I flicked my wrist, and the chain snapped with a metallic clang, saving what little living metal I had left from burning. The False Angel cackled, dropping the burning pieces onto the ground below her. The flame spread fast, consuming whatever it touched. That awful voice rang out again.

"Poor little human, not enough to make a single weapon."

She floated back down in front of me, those black wings wrapping around us. The fire cloaked her face in shadow, hiding the monstrosity as she leaned in close.

"Come now, I'm sorry for hurting your feelings. I just wanted a toy. Heeey, what if I let you pick the next toy? Would you forgive me then?"

She forced me to the floor, trapping me under her talons, before I could tell her to fuck off. Another tittering manic laugh bubbled out of her mouth. "JK. LOL. Smiley face. I pick the toys. But if you're good, I might let you watch me play."

Zarael's talons sank into my shoulder, and I winced as she kicked me away. I slid across the floor. I could feel the coldness of the blade against my skin before slamming into it. A wide grin spread across her face, tearing it in half. What remained hung off of her crown, barely disguising the writhing mass of muscle beneath it.

"Oopsie, hope nothing bad happens if I turn my back."

She spun around and watched the fire, occasionally glancing over her shoulder. I saw her game. I could play along. The living metal dripped down the sword as I grabbed it, coating the blade. I pulled it from the earth and charged at The False Angel, screaming my intention at her. She let out a grunt as the sword pierced her back and pushed out through her chest. Her head spun around to face me.

"Got it out of your system yet?"

I grinned at her, staring into those putrid eyes. "Something like that. Consume."

In an emergency, the living metal could replicate and make more of itself. But it needed fuel. The one time I tried it before, the metal had to eat a sedan just to form the base suit. But now it had a self-replicating parasite, practically a buffet.

The False Angel shrieked in pain, an unnatural sound that filled the room and cracked the windows. I could feel blood drip from my ears. Her scream was cut off as the living metal poured out of her mouth, then each ear and onto her shoulders, dissolving whatever it came into contact with. Each part of her that melted away tried to reform, only to be consumed again as the living metal fed. Her body shifted wildly, adding more limbs, growing rapidly and randomly to escape my black plague. I backed away as her body writhed, threatening to strike me. But each blow was eaten away. Her body shrank, melting into a skeletal figure that hobbled along the floor, grasping after me. And then, with a final pathetic wheeze, The False Angel melted into nothing.

I gazed up at the black, writhing mass of living metal, suspended in the air above me, and marveled at how much there was. I let it flow over me, basking in its icy embrace. My armor formed, more massive than it had ever been. Thick metal plate shielded me, black spikes shooting up with each movement. It felt like I was covered in pure muscle, flexing and hardening. My cape stretched out behind me, the ragged fabric writhing almost like a set of demonic wings. A hood fell over my face, making sure no human features were seen. The living metal had a presence now, a sort of sentience that lived up to its name. And still, there was more it could do, more it could make. A wicked, curving scythe formed in my hands. I stared at it, excited by the possibility. I had told Zarael in a dream once, I would raze this world to the ground if I ever lost her. Now here was my chance.

Red and blue lights flashed outside, beckoning me to meet them. I rushed the doors, grasping the blade that would cleave the world in twain at my side. The cathedral doors burst open, flying off their ancient hinges. A handful of police cars formed a semicircle around me. All that was left in the city, unprepared to meet this brand-new Malice. The cathedral burned behind me, flames hissing as the rain struck them. I stepped forward, letting my massive new suit crack the steps beneath me.

And I…

I…

I was tired. All the rage, every scrap of anger that had pushed me through the night, fighting off exhaustion and fatigue, flowed out of me. I just felt…empty. It had all been directed at The False Angel, and now she was gone. I won. Everything that I had been angry about before she arrived seemed pointless now. Silly. Why was I so angry all the time?

I looked out at the cops surrounding me, saw the fear painted across their faces. Was this what I wanted? Fear? Destruction? No, I set out to fix the world. I wanted to make it better. Maybe Zarael, the real one, had been right. Maybe it was time for a change.

I didn't want to be angry anymore, to be guided solely by rage.

I knelt on the ground, throwing down the scythe. I tried to push away the suit, let it melt around me. It was reluctant. Tried to cling on to me. Strange new behavior. But I was able to coax it away, let it leave me undefended. I held my hands in the air, watching as one officer slowly approached me. He kept his hands at his side and knelt down to look at me.

"What's your name, son?"

"Mal—" I started to answer him, but no. Malice was dead. He died with The False Angel.

"Dante. My name is Dante."

About the Author

Kaden Conorich is a Cryptid-In-Training living in Hellishly hot California, just waiting for his chance to disappear into a forest and reappear in children's nightmares. But for now he's writing horror. Starcrossed is his first book.